THE MURDERESS

The Murderess

ALEXANDROS PAPADIAMANTIS

Translated from the Greek by Peter Levi

Writers and Readers

London   New York

Writers and Readers Publishing Cooperative Society Ltd
144 Camden High Street, London NW1 0NE
England

This English translation published by Writers and Readers
Publishing Cooperative Ltd. 1983

Cover Design Jacque Solomons

Typeset in Garamond by Inforum Ltd, Portsmouth
Printed in Great Britain by Billing & Sons Ltd., Worcester

ISBN 0 904613 94 1 Cloth

'Writers and Readers gratefully acknowledge the assistance of the
Arts Council of Great Britain in the translation of this book.'

ALEXANDROS PAPADIAMANTIS is often thought of as the greatest of modern Greek prose writers. He was born on the small rocky island of Skiathos in the northern Sporades on 4 March 1851 to a family priestly on his father's side, and made up of seamen and landowners on his mother's side. Because of the family's straitened circumstances, he left school at the age of twelve and spent the next four years studying French and English on his own and roaming the island which was to remain the source of his inspiration. At the age of sixteen, he was sent to high school in Chalkis. From there he went to the monastic community on Mount Athos where he acquired a profound knowledge of church ritual and Byzantine psalmody, the second source of his literary inspiration. But he decided against taking vows and went instead to Athens to finish high school and then enrol at university. He earned his keep by doing journalism and translation, but his meagre funds – further diminished by money he had to send home – prevented him from taking a degree. Two early novels brought him some recognition and it was then that he began writing those remarkable stories and novellas which gained him a unique place in European letters. Papadiamantis was appalled by the corruption of government, the lax morals of a society to whose worldliness he was ill-fitted. He shunned all publicity and few people who met the tall man with the bristly black beard and shabby overcoat knew who he was. Overwork, heavy smoking and drinking gradually undermined his health and he returned to the tranquillity of his beloved island where he died on 3 January 1911.

For Deirdre

Translator's Introduction

Most of us who love reading began early. We were possessed before we realized it by a hungry curiosity about the world. So it is small wonder that the regional novel has always had a special place in our affections. I suppose such novels must exist by now in every written language. Walter Scott may have been the source of the tradition, but in many of the later examples the historical impetus of Scott's novels is lacking. They concentrate rather on local antiquities and local colour, but they have their kind of truth, and at best they convey powerfully the nature and quality of some dead provincial world. When such a novel captures an important crisis of the past, it may be the best instrument we have to understand the present. That is the least that can be said of *The Murderess*.

In some ways Papadiamantis was a very naive writer. In his style the many mingled elements, the genuine folklore and the dryads in which he all but believes, the realism and the exoticism, the narrative gift and the excessively romantic lyricism, make it impossible to disentangle his virtues from his vices as a writer. They are also extremely hard to render in modern English. His language and tone have many changes. He is a parodist and a satirist and also a recorder of dialect. He belongs uniquely to a particular moment in Greek development, in the troubled history of the Greek language and the first emergence of its modern literature. At the same time he is inevitably the civilized observer of a retarded world. Athens in the nineties was not London or Paris, though one can smell in his writing more than a whiff of European influence from the mid-century, but the island world that Papadiamantis described was provincial in a far deeper sense. Skiathos was fifty times further behind the Athens of that time than Athens was behind Paris or London.

This novel makes it clear that Papadiamantis wrote about a world to which he was born, an island of which he knew every stick and stone, every legend and every piece of gossip. For most of us that passionate genuineness does an important service. It fills with realism and with thrilling interest the somewhat shadowy period of early modern Greek history. But that is not the point of the book, any more than the similar service that Thomas Hardy does in English — and for which today we greatly value, even overvalue, his novels — provided the momentum of *Tess* or of *Jude the Obscure*. In fact Hardy and Papadiamantis in their different spheres have a striking number of elements in common, even to the extent of a certain necessary awkwardness and naivety.

The motive force of *The Murderess* is certainly to be found in the history and the tragic paradox of the central character. Papadiamantis was a religious man; he had tried his vocation as a monk on Athos. But no religious solution is offered. Religion in this novel is used simply to deepen the tragic tone. Nor is any human or secular solution offered. What happens, with the whole weight of what leads to it, is like a wild scream of protest. Is the murderess mad? Sleepless, worn out by life, half-mad in the end, exalted by madness only as a tragic heroine is exalted. I assume that Papadiamantis knew the Medea of Euripides as well as he knew nineteenth-century novelists.

The mechanism of the story is quite simple. Papadiamantis was a magnificent writer of short stories and essentially this is a very long short story. The old woman, whose background and whose whole life are made clear to us with an economy that one notices only in retrospect, is driven to despair about the fate of women in Greek island communities like her own. Girls are such a burden to their mothers they would really be better dead. Papadiamantis writes with particular horror of the dowry system, which incidentally has not died to this day. We are led to consider back street abortions, superstitions, the lack of doctors, the idiocy of officials, the corruption of the new, 'liberated' middle class, and the fate of poor families. Greece has altered of course, but a lot of this is still recognizable, at least in remote places. But the key of the story is the obligation on the poorest women and the poorest families to scrape together marriage settlements for every girl born.

Social progress is not offered as a palliative. Indeed it is progress which has done some of the harm. Earlier or later in history there might be different problems: the tax officers take over from the bandits, and the local girls 'take on confidence', without learning anything at school. At this given moment, the old woman is ground between an upper and a lower millstone. Maybe the monks in their monastery are happy, because they bring no children into the world? Not even Papadiamantis can really believe that. It was a passing thought, like the aspiration to fly away like a bird and be at peace. The hermit on his rock and the monastic gardener with his verses from the psalm are like similar figures in Shakespeare. They define a world, they may even play a role, but they are not really characters in the same sense as those that human passion haunts.

It has been impossible to produce accurately the texture of the original. I had trouble with proverbs and the names of herbs. Certain popular phrases exist in every language that have roots in an entire culture, and Papadiamantis uses more of them than most writers. Then at times he can be painfully slow and repetitive, or he can drag in by the hair some weighty phrase out of a literary journal. Nowadays a publisher's editor would simply strike it out. It is not the task of a mere translator to underline such phrases. At times I have been forced by over-riding considerations of clarity to speed them up, and five or six times I have reorganized entire sentences. They were usually the kind of sentence that runs, 'The clouds in the sky . . .' and then five lines later, 'the clouds, as I was saying . . .' It is not fair to Papadiamantis to reproduce such sentences today in English unless one could be quite certain that the translation was no worse than its original. There is a leisure about Papadiamantis, an ease inside his own skin, which is hard to recapture.

It extends beyond these lengthy and relaxed passages to his great set pieces, the ruined chapel and the sea-eagle's nest, the old woman's dreams and the devil-dance of the stones. They remind me personally of the great set pieces in Dickens which I neither could nor would like to imitate: 'What are the wild waves saying?' for example. They seem to be in a different category from the extravagant improbabilities of the plot. In those one can almost believe, because of the constant tang of reality, and because of the real force of the central tragedy. But the set pieces have a function of their own. It is something to do with the relief of pressure. The story builds up such a head of steam that without these literary escapes through metaphor, whose function is to calm it or temper it, I do not see how it could proceed. But these are subjective criticisms. The ultimate set piece is the end of the novel, and that surely is perfectly timed. I find it brilliant, enthralling, and unforgettable.

It is a long time since I first came across this novel. What was once my respectful curiosity has become a deeper wonder. For that I owe thanks to the publishers for pushing me into translating it. I also owe lasting gratitude to Ian Watson, who loves Papadiamantis and who in casual conversation greatly increased my feeling for his style. Most of all I must thank John Berger, who noticed *The Murderess* in a French translation, and insisted on its merits and on its modern interest. He also helped me out of a difficult impasse when I was unable to hit on a style for this version, by producing several pages of silk purse out of several pages of sow's ear.

PETER LEVI
STONESFIELD
1981

1

Old Hadoula, sometimes known as Jannis Frankissa, lay beside the hearth, with her eyes closed and her head resting on the step of the fireplace, the cinder-step as it is known. She had not dozed off, she was giving up her sleep at the cradle of her sick grand-daughter. As for the new mother, who had given birth to the sick child, she had been sound asleep for a little while now in her unhappy nest on the floor.

The little hanging lamp guttered under the canopy of the fireplace. It threw shadows instead of light on the few miserable sticks of furniture, which looked cleaner and grander at night than in the daytime. The three half-burnt logs and the big upright balk of timber in the hearth made a lot of ash, a few glowing cinders and a flame that crackled quietly and reminded the old woman through her drowsiness of her absent younger daughter Krinio. If Krinio had been in the house now she would have been whispering in a low chant, 'If he's a friend good luck to him, and if he isn't, damn him.'

Hadoula, or Frankissa, or Frankojannou, was a woman of scarcely sixty, well built and solid, with a masculine air and two little touches of moustache on her lips. In her private thoughts, when she summed up her entire life, she saw that she had never done anything except serve others. When she was a little girl, she had served her parents. When she was mated, she became a slave to her husband, and at the same time, because of her strength and his weakness, she was his nurse. When she had children she became a slave to her

1

children, and when they had children of their own, she was slave to her grandchildren.

The baby had been born two weeks ago. It had been a difficult birth. The mother was Frankojannou's eldest daughter, Delcharo Trahilaina, who lay sleeping now. They had been forced to baptize the child on the tenth day, since she was seriously ill. She had a bad cough, a rash, and something like convulsions. After baptism, the baby seemed to improve a little on the first evening, and the coughing relaxed for a while. For many nights Frankojannou had permitted herself no sleep. She had willed her sore eyes open, while she kept vigil beside this little creature who had no idea what trouble she was giving, or what tortures she must undergo in her turn, if she survived. Nor was she capable of feeling the despair to which her grandmother only secretly gave expression: 'O God, why should another one come into the world?'

As the old woman rocked the child, she could have sung the whole saga of her sufferings over the cradle. In the course of the previous nights she had really lost track of reason in the catalogue of her sufferings. The whole of her life, with its futility and its emptiness and hardness, had come into her mind in pictures and scenes, and in visions.

Her father was thrifty, hard-working and sensible; her mother was wicked and blasphemous and envious. She was one of the witches of those days. She knew magic. Two or three times the outlaws had driven her away, the fighting men of Karatasos and Gatsos and the other Macedonian captains. They did so to take their vengeance, because she had used magic on them and their affairs had not prospered. For three months they had idled away their time, unable to take loot from Turk or Christian. Nor had the Government in Corinth sent them any help.

They had driven her from the crest of Saint Thanasi down to the plateau of Prophet Elias, with its enormous plane trees and abundant springs, and from there to Merovili on the mountainside, through brushwood and mountain thickets. She tried to hide herself in the deep thicket, but they were not fooled. The rustle of leaves and branches, and her own trembling which made the bushes and the briars shake, betrayed her. It was then she heard the brutal voice:

'Ah, little girl, so we've got you!'

She leapt away through the bushes and ran off like a frightened dove, her big white sleeves flapping like wings. Yet there was no hope of escape. Once before, the first time they had hunted her, she had managed to hide, but that was down at Pyrgi where there were so many different paths. Here at Merovili there were no such tracks, no such mazes, nothing but groves of trees and dense, impassable thickets.

Delcharao, Frankojannou's mother, was still young then, and she leapt like a deer from bush to bush, barefooted, because she had long ago thrown off her shoes — one of her pursuers had taken one of them for spoils — and now the thorns stuck in her heels and tore and bloodied her ankles and her calves. Then, in her despair, inspiration came to her. Over on that side of the thicket, on the slope of the mountainside, there was a single cultivated olive-grove, called Moraitis' Pine. Old Moraitis, who was the father of the owner, had migrated there from Mystra around the end of the last century, in the times of Catherine of Russia and the Orlov expedition. The famous pine-tree stood in the middle of the olives like a giant among dwarfs. It was a thousand years old, and at the foot of its gigantic trunk, which five men's arms could not encompass, it was hollowed out. The shepherds and fishermen had dug into it, they had cut away its heart and hollowed out its inside to take fuel, and it had yielded plenty. With this terrible wound in its guts, the pine tree lived on for another three-quarters of a century, until 1871. In July of that year, people who lived miles away down by the sea felt a severe local earthquake. That night the giant tree had crashed.

It was into that hollow, where two men could have sat easily, that the newly married Delcharo, who was to be the mother of Frankojannou, ran to hide. It was a desperate, almost a childish expedient. She was hidden there only in her own imagination, like a child playing hide and seek. Her pursuers would certainly see her, discover her hiding-place. She was invisible only from the back, not from the front. As soon as the three outlaws got beyond the pine-tree, they would see her crouching down in the hollow.

The three men came running, they were passing her, they went on running. Two of them did not even turn round. They imagined she was running on ahead. Just at the last moment, the third one turned as if he had been shot. He looked backwards in every direction except towards the trunk of the pine tree. Or rather he did notice the tree vaguely among other things, but without guessing that its trunk had a hollow in which someone might hide. Whether he knew of the hollow in that gigantic trunk or not, at that moment no thought of it entered his head. He was looking for a hole in the ground that might have swallowed her up. But there was not so much as a wrinkle in the earth for anyone to hide in. The dryads, the forest nymphs whom she perhaps invoked in her magic, were protecting her, they were blinding her pursuers, they were laying a leaf-coloured mist, a green darkness over their eyes – and they failed to see her.

The young woman was saved from her pursuers' clutches. And from that day she went on working her magic, her spells against the outlaws, bringing frustration into their affairs, so that they could find no more loot anywhere – until the time when by God's grace things quietened down, and Sultan Mahmout made over the Devil's Islands to Greece. They then ceased to be exempt from taxes. Taxation took over from looting, and ever since then the whole beloved people has continued to labour for a vast central stomach which has no ears.

4

Hadoula Frankissa had been born by then, though she was very small, and she later remembered everything her mother told her. Then when she grew up and came to be seventeen and things were a little more peaceful, in the days of the Governor Capodistria, her parents married her off to a man called Iannis Frankos. This husband she referred to as 'the Hat', and as 'the Bill'.

The titles Hadoula gave her man were not without foundation. She called him Hat even before she was married, when she used to tease him with girlish spite — without foreseeing that he was going to be her fate and her lover — because instead of a fez he wore a kind of long cinder-red bonnet with a little pompom. The Bill was a name she gave him later, after she was married, because he had the habit of saying 'That's how the bill adds up,' although he was unable himself to add up even a few halfpence or two days' wages. If she had not been there, they would have tricked him every day. They would never have given him the right wages for his work on the boats, at the dry docks or in the boat yard, where he laboured as a carpenter and a fitter.

For a long time he had been an apprentice and assistant to her father, who had followed the same trade. When the old man noticed the young man's simplicity, his economy and his modesty, he respected him for it and resolved to make him a son-in-law. As a dowry, he offered him a deserted, tumbledown house in the old Castle, where people used to live once upon a time, before the '21 revolution. He also gave him a so-called kitchen garden which was just outside the deserted Castle, on a precipitous bit of the coast, three hours away from the modern town. He threw in a field the size of a handkerchief, a bit of wild land which the neighbour was going to claim was his, while the other neighbours maintained that both the fields the two of them were quarrelling about were stolen, being really Church property from an abandoned monastery. That was the sort of dowry old

Statharos gave his daughter. And she was an only daughter. He kept for himself and his wife and son the newly constructed houses in the modern town, the two vineyards near it, two olive groves, some fields, and whatever valuables he possessed.

That was the point Frankojannou's recollections had reached on the night in question. It was the eleventh night since the birth. The baby girl had had a relapse, and was suffering terribly. She had come ill into the world. The decline had already begun in her mother's womb.

At that moment the baby broke into a fit of coughing, and Frankojannou's waking dreams and memories were interrupted. She shifted on the miserable couch where she lay, leant over the child and tried to comfort it as best she could. She held a small flask up into the light, and attempted to put a spoonful to the baby's lips. The child tasted the liquid and a moment later spat it out again.

The mother stirred on her low, narrow bed. It seemed she was not sleeping well. She was merely dozing with her eyes shut. She opened them now, raised her head two or three inches, and asked,

'How is she, mother?'

'How do you think she is?' said the old woman grimly. 'Now you lie quiet as well! What's she to do? Can't she cough?'

'What do you think, mother?'

'What am I to think? She's a tiny mite of a baby . . . there you are, another little atom come into the world!' The old woman spoke the phrase in a strange and bitter tone.

Soon the mother was sleeping more quietly. At the break of dawn, after the third crowing of the cock, the old woman shut her eyes for a little while. She was woken by the voice of Amersa, her other daughter, who had come over from the little house nearby, impatient to know how the young mother and the baby were doing and how the night had

6

passed for her own mother.

Amersa was the second daughter, unmarried, an old maid already, although she was an industrious, capable workwoman, famous for her sewing. She was tall and dark and mannish. Her trousseau and the embroideries that she had made had been shut away for many years in a big unpolished chest where moth and worm nibbled at them.

'Good morning. How are you? How was it?'

'Is it you Amersa? There, that's another night gone.'

The old woman had just woken and was rubbing her eyes and yawning. A noise came from the little room next door. It was Dadis Trahilis, husband of the young mother, who slept at the other side of the thin wooden partition, with another little girl and a tiny boy; he had just that minute woken. He was getting together his tools, saws and hammers and planes, and preparing to go to the boatyard for his day's work.

'Listen to the clatter he makes!' said the old woman. 'He can't get his tools together without making a noise. Anyone who hears him knows what's going on!'

'You cannot build a gypsy's house . . .' said Amersa with an ironic laugh.

The noise the unseen Dadis made behind the partition as he flung his tools – hammer, saws, augers, and so on – one by one into his bag finally woke his wife.

'What's happening, mother?'

'What do you think? Konstantis is throwing his things into his bag!' answered the old lady with a sigh.

' . . . and you measure his money out of ash,' Amersa finished the proverb.

Suddenly the voice of Konstantis came through the flimsy partition.

'Are you awake, mother-in-law?' he said. 'How did you get on?'

'How should we get on! Like the hen in the millrace. Come and drink your raki.'

Dadis appeared at the door of the winter room. He was broadchested, awkwardly built, 'like nothing on earth' as his old mother-in-law used to say, and nearly bald. The old woman showed Amersa the little raki bottle on the shelf above the hearth, and nodded to her to pour a small glass for Konstantis to drink.

'Isn't there a fig anywhere?' he asked, as he took the raki glass from his sister-in-law's hand.

'Where would such a thing be found?' said old Hadoula. 'We need forty cinder-cakes here,' she added. She was referring to the money it was normal to spend even in poorer houses at the time of such a 'happy event' as the birth of a daughter.

'Do you want a son-in-law who has eyes?' said Amersa, remembering another proverb.

'Perhaps you'd prefer a toothless one,' Dadis replied, without turning a hair, and then added an even more obscure proverb. 'Eviva! Happy fortieth day!'

He drank down the thick liquid in the little glass without drawing breath.

'Good day to you.'

He picked up his bag and set off for the yard.

2

The fire was going out in the hearth, the lamp was guttering under the small chimney, the mother was dozing on the bed, the infant was coughing in the cradle, and Frankojannou lay awake on her couch, as she had done night after night.

It was about the first crowing of the cock, when memories arise like ghosts. After they had married her off and installed her, and endowed her with the tumbledown house at the old uninhabitable Castle, and the kitchen garden on the wild north headland, and the bit of wild ground disputed by the neighbour and by the Monastery, the bride settled down with her husband in the house of his sister, who was a widow. There she set up her own household with a few small possessions. The dowry contract stated in detail that she was given so many changes of clothes, so many shirts, so many cushions, with two metal pots, one pan, one potstand, and so on. The contract itemized even the knives and forks and spoons.

Her husband's widowed sister went through everything on the Monday immediately following the wedding, and found that two sheets, two pillows, one pot, and one complete change of clothes were missing from the list. That same day she told her brother's mother-in-law to supply the missing items. The avaricious old woman replied that what she had given was given in good spirit, and that was enough. So the sister-in-law berated her brother, and he complained to the bride, who answered, 'If you were awake to your own interest, you would not have accepted a house at the Castle

9

where nothing lives but ghosts and what use are sheets and shirts to you, when you're not capable of getting a house and a vineyard and an olive-grove?'

Hadoula had genuinely tried to whisper something like this into her fiancé's ears at the time of their engagement. Young as she was, she was nonetheless extremely cunning and devious, thanks to nature and to her mother's conscious and unconscious example. But her mother got wind of her schemes and for fear that the little Witch, as she was accustomed to refer to her daughter, might excite the wits of her fiancé to intrigue for a bigger dowry, the old lady had exercised a tyrannical supervision over the engaged couple, not permitting the slightest private conversation between them. She did this under the pretence of severe propriety.

'I won't have that little Witch building me a bastard,' she had said.

You can see that she took her metaphor from her husband's boat-building trade. But she really said it so as not to be compelled to give a bigger dowry.

One evening, the day before the engagement, the bride-groom and his sister had come to the house to discuss the dowry. The old boatmaker dictated the contract to Sybias, the Reader, who was also the chanter from the local church. Sybias had taken his brass inkwell from his belt, and his goose-feather pen from its long holder in the inkwell, which was rather like a pistol. He had put the book of the Holy Apostle on his knees, and a bit of thick paper on the book, and had written at the old man's dictation, 'In the Name of the Father and of the Son and of the Holy Spirit . . . I marry my daughter Hadoula to Iannis Frankos, and I give her first of all my blessing.' Hadoula stood opposite the hearth, next to the pile of blankets and covers and cushions, covered with a silken sheet and curling up into two enormous cushions; she looked as motionless and grandiose as the pile of linen, but all the same she nodded impatiently yet circumspectly to her

10

fiancé and to his sister, not to accept 'house at the Castle' and 'field at Stoiboto' for a dowry, but to ask for a house in the new town, and a vineyard and an olive grove in the same neighbourhood.

In vain. Neither her fiancé nor his sister noticed her desperate nods. Only her mother, who — although she was compelled to turn her back on her daughter in order politely to face her new son-in-law and his sister — had contrived to sit with only one shoulder turned away, twisted round as suddenly as if an invisible spirit had told her that something was up. She saw the forbidden mimicry.

She shot a ferociously threatening glance at Hadoula.

'Ah, my little witch,' she whispered to herself, 'be careful or I shall fix you.'

But almost at once she realized it was not in her own interest to have words with her daughter over the dowry. She must give her no excuse to complain to her father. That would certainly make matters worse. The old man would probably yield to the weepings and beseechings of his only daughter and give her a bigger dowry. So the mother kept quiet.

As soon as they were alone, Hadoula was amazed that, although her mother had clearly seen her making those dangerous nods, for the first time in her life she didn't scratch her, or pinch her, or bite her, as she usually did. It should be said that the dowry gift of a house in the old, uninhabitable village had some justification. A lot of houses were still left standing at the Castle, and some families used to spend the summer up there. Then, too, people had a prejudice in favour of the Old Village. The old folks lamented leaving it, they had not yet got used to the new order of things, or to this peaceful life without attacks from outlaws or pirates or the Turkish armada. Their settling in the new town was not considered definitive. There lingered a feeling that people would be forced in the end to go back to their old ways and

11

their cautious habits. Yet although they were always recalling the Castle and grieving for the Castle and dreaming of the Castle, and although it was always on their lips, that did not stop them building houses in the new housing area, proving for the ten thousandth time that people are accustomed to think one thing and do another, in simple mechanical imitation of each other.

So two weeks after the engagement, the marriage took place. That was how the bride's mother wanted it. She had no wish, as she said, for an unmarried son-in-law to be hanging about the house; he was quite bold enough already, as a fellow-craftsman and a hanger-on of her husband. The bridegroom's elderly widowed sister, who had one fully grown son working at the boatyard, as well as a younger boy and girl, took the new couple into her house. A year later the first boy, Stathis, was born, then Delcharo, afterwards Yalis, later Michalis, after that Amersa, and after her Mitrakis, and last of all Krinio.

In the early days peace appeared to reign in the house. Then, when the bride's two first children had begun to grow and her sister-in-law's two youngest were already grown up, civil war broke out. Frankojannou, who had become much wiser with age and experience of the world, had achieved the purchase of a house of her own, thanks to her own cleverness and thrift, as she modestly remarked. The first year all she could build was four mudbrick walls, thin and not high, with a roof on them. The second year she floored three quarters of the house, that is, she made a little floor with a variety of uneven planks, old and new. Then losing no time, impatient to be liberated from the tyrannical rule of her aging and increasingly eccentric sister-in-law, she packed herself up and moved, and set up house with her husband and children in her 'little corner', in her 'nest', in her 'refuge'. On that day, as she used to say, she felt the greatest joy of 'all her days'.

In those long, sleepless January nights, Frankojannou

remembered and relived all these things. The north wind could be heard whistling outside, rattling the tiles and making the windows echo, while she kept her vigil by the cradle of her grandchild. It was the third hour after midnight, and the cock crowed again. The little girl, who has just quietened down a few minutes ago, started to cough painfully again. She had come into this world weak, and on top of that had caught cold on the third day in her bath, a big wooden tub. The result was a bad cough. For days now Frankojannou had been watching anxiously for symptoms of convulsion in the weak little creature — because then she knew she could not survive — but fortunately she observed nothing of the kind. 'She's there to be tortured and to torture us,' she had whispered to herself without being overheard.

Frankojannou opened her sleepless eyes and rocked the cradle. She wanted to give the suffering infant the usual drink.

'Who's coughing?' asked a voice beyond the partition.

The old woman did not answer. It was Saturday night, and her son-in-law had drunk an extra raki before supper, and after supper a big glass of clear wine to refresh himself from the whole working week. So having had enough to drink, Dadis now spoke or rather rambled in his sleep.

The baby would not take the spoonful of drink; she pushed it away with her tongue as she coughed. The cough was very much worse.

'Shut up,' said the child's father, still in his sleep.

'And belt up,' Frankojannou added ironically.

The mother suddenly woke; maybe she heard the child's cough and the angry little exchange through the partition.

'What is it mother?' said Delcharo, getting up. 'Is the child not well?'

The old woman smiled grimly in the trembling light of the little lamp.

'You haven't said the half of it, daughter,' she said angrily.

13

It was not the first time her daughter had heard her talk like that. She remembered other times when her mother had expressed herself with a meaningful shake of the head to the women and the old crones of the neighbourhood as they discussed the great superfluity of young girls, the rarity of young men, their journeys abroad, their huge demands for dowries and all the tortures a Christian woman went through to establish her 'weaker vessels'. During discussions of that kind Hadoula uttered similar sentiments. Particularly when she heard of the illnesses of little girls, she had been heard to say, with a shake of her head:

'You haven't said the half of it. Is there no death? Are there no rocks to expose them on?' She would often use such over-expressive language. Another time she was heard to assert that it wasn't in a person's interest to have a lot of daughters, and the best things was not to be married at all. Her accustomed prayer for little girls was 'May they not survive! May they go no further!'

On occasion she went so far as to say:

'What can I say to you! . . . The minute girls are born a person thinks of strangling them!'

Yes, she did say it, but she would certainly never have been capable of doing it, Not even Hadoula herself believed that.

3

Night after night had flowed past in the same way since the birth of the child. The baby had been baptized and named Hadoula after its grandmother, which made that lady grimace and shake her head and mutter, 'In case the name should die out!' Now the old woman was awake again, even though the baby seemed to be somewhat calmer. Sleeplessness was in Frankojannou's nature and in her temperament. She thought over a thousand things, and sleep did not come to her easily. Her ponderings and memories, dim images of the past, arose in her mind one after the other like waves that her soul could see.

Hadoula had brought so many children into the world, and she had built a little house to live in. The more the family increased, the more the bitter pills multiplied. She had obtained her little house by her own economies, not from her husband's savings. Iannis the craftsman, the Hat or the Bill, did not really know how to calculate: not even how many days' wages were due to him, nor how much four or five or six days a week would come to at one seventy-five or one eighty, those being his wages as a third class carpenter. Sometimes he was paid as a finisher at two thirty-five or two forty, but even then he was still incapable of adding it up.

He just liked to drink it, nearly all of it, on Sundays. Except that his wife fortunately took her precautions, and had the money in her own hands by Saturday night. Or sometimes she drew it straight from the foreman, not without problems and disputes, since the foreman disliked

15

handing it over to her, preferring to deal with Iannis himself, from whom of course he retained ten or fifteen farthings, as he did from all the others, as a special percentage, saying 'I have daughters, comrade, I have daughters.' But Frankojannou was not going to be fooled. She gave him back the only logical and the only proper reply: 'Are you the only one who has daughters, Master? Has the rest of the world got none?'

Or if she failed to get the money from the master boat-builder, then she snatched it, half-jokingly but not quite in jest, out of her husband's hands. Of course she took care to soften him up first and put him in the right mood. Or else she let him fall asleep at last, half-drunk, and stole the money from his pockets on Saturday night. On Sunday morning she just gave him forty or fifty farthings for pocket-money.

So she had built the little house by her economies. But what was the first foundation of that small capital sum? At that moment in the sleepless night she admitted it to herself for the first time. She had never mentioned it even in confession, where anyway she used to confess only very small things, just the usual sins that the priest knew before she said them: malicious gossip, anger, women's bad language and so on. She had never confessed to her mother in her mother's lifetime, though she had been the only person to suspect the truth without even being told it. It was true she had tried, and she had decided to tell her in her last moments. But unhappily, before her death the old woman became deaf, dumb and unconcious, 'like an object,' as her daughter described her condition, so Hadoula had had no opportunity of confessing her sin.

Still less did she tell her father or her husband. Her secret was this.

Before her marriage Hadoula had begun to steal, little by little, from her father's money. A few farthings here, a half-penny there. So little that he hardly noticed, and never became suspicious. He kept his treasury in a hiding-place that his wife had discovered long ago, and Hadoula in time had discovered it too. Only on two occasions did he remark that his estimate of his tiny treasury must have been mistaken. Hadoula stopped her thefts for the time being, so as not to let her father's suspicion grow. Later she began to steal again, more and more; but compared to her mother's thieving she was a novice.

The mother had stolen a lot, never without skill and method. She stole mostly from those special enterprises which she managed herself, like the sale of oil and wine produced from family land, and she also took a little, hardly as much as her daughter, from her husband's wages. As time went by and work increased, old Stathis became a small foreman himself building boats and kaikis on his own in the forecourt of his house, helped only by his son and his apprentice. The old woman was then able to steal considerable sums from the boat-building as well.

A few months before her marriage, young Hadoula had succeeded in discovering the hiding-place where her mother kept her hoard. In a corner of the cellar, among the half-filled pots and the empty barrels, was a long, fat bundle of black kerchiefs in which the old lady had tied up as many as a hundred and seventy silver coins, jumbled up like a pack of dogs in the street, some Spanish, some Italian and some Turkish, all stolen from the old man's income and the produce of their land. Hadoula had counted the jumble of coins with amazement and excitement. She was shaking with emotion, then she put away the coins in their corner without the courage to disturb them any more.

But on the eve of her marriage, after she had seen her parents' obstinacy, their refusal to give her a sufficient dowry, and recognized her mother's cruelty, she waited for a moment when the old woman would leave the house for a while, and then with a shaking heart she secretly went down into the cellar. She felt for the hoard and found it. She untied it. This time it seemed to her small. She had no time for counting. Maybe the old woman had taken some of the silver pieces and used them for who knows what purpose. It came into her mind that she might take the whole bundle, wrapped in her mother's old kerchief, but she was afraid. She took only eight or nine pieces for a start, as many as she imagined would not make much difference to the size of the bundle, and would not be noticeable at once. She went to retie the kerchief, but then she opened it out again and took another five or six, fifteen coins in all. And then again as she tied the knot, the desire came over her to undo it once more, to take just two or three more pieces. Suddenly she heard her mother's footsteps outside. She hastily did up the bundle and put it back in its place.

The old woman discovered the theft a few days after the marriage. But she was unwilling to say anything to her daughter. She was thankful she had not taken the lot. 'She was blinded,' she muttered between her teeth.

That sum which Hadoula had stolen long ago from her parents, amounting to about four hundred bits in the coinage of those days, she hid carefully for many years. In order to build the house she increased it by her own resourcefulness. She was hardworking and she was skilful. So far as the cares of rearing so many children one on top of another permitted it, she went out to work. In small places 'there are no specialists, only general trades'. The village grocer is also the outfitter and the chemist and a credit company as well. So there was nothing to prevent a good needlewoman, as Frankojannou was, from acting the nurse or the doctor or anything else as long as she was adaptable. And Frankojannou was the most adaptable of all women.

She provided herbs, she made ointments, she gave massages, she cured the evil eye, she put together medicine for the sick, for anaemic girls, for pregnant women and women after childbirth and for those with women's diseases.

18

With her basket swinging on her left arm, and with the two smallest children trailing after her, Dimitraki who was eight, and Krinio who was six, she went out into the fields and up into the mountains, across ravines and valleys and rivers, in search of plants that she knew, wild onion, dragon-weed, thirdweed and others. She cut them or uprooted them and so she filled her basket and came home as the day ended.

With these herbs she prepared various tonics which she maintained were sovereign remedies against chronic diseases of the chest or the womb or the stomach. These various resources, together with thrift, led to small profits and in time she succeeded in building her little nest. But the young birds had already begun to spread their wings, and fly away overseas.

At that time her eldest son Statharos was already twenty years old and overseas in America. After two or three letters he had fallen silent, giving no further sign of life. Three years later her second son Yalis had gown up in his turn and taken ship.

Both of them in their early years had tried their father's trade, but neither the one nor the other made much progress, and they were neither of them satisfied. As an affectionate son and brother, Yalis wrote to his mother from Marseilles, where he had travelled with a Greek ship, to say that he too had decided to go to America, to see what had become of his elder brother, and maybe find him somewhere. But year after year had gone by since then and no more had been heard of either of them.

Their mother used that occasion to remember one of the funnier of the popular folktales, which tells of a honey-mine, in which first the old woman's eldest son, who was sent to fetch the honey, got stuck; and then her second, who was sent in to unstick the first, got stuck; and then the third, who was sent to bring back the other two, got stuck; and finally the Old Man, who went to see what had become of his sons, he got stuck as well. They all got stuck. And in the end the Old Woman decided to go and see for herself what had become of her Old Man and the children, since they never came home from the quest she sent them on. Being a cunning old woman, she looked on from a distance and she was the only one to escape and not get stuck. So she turned to the four of them stuck in the honey-mine and she said, 'You mined honey, but I never mined.'

Meanwhile, during the time that Statharos and Yalis had gone overseas to America and eaten the flower of the lotus or drunk the waters of Lethe, Delcharo, the eldest daughter and first child after the two travelling brothers, was growing up. It seemed to happen all at once. And Amersa, hardly four years younger than her sister, was growing up at the same rate, and putting on height. She was becoming mannish, dark and energetic, and the women of the neighbourhood called her the manwoman. And even the little one, Krinaki, who lacked (alas) the colour of the lily of her name, although she was slim by nature, was showing signs of development.

'My God, how they grow!' thought Frankojannou. What garden, what meadow, what springtime produced this plant? And how it thrives and flowers and puts out leaves and establishes itself! And will all these shoots, every budding plant, grow to greens and lawns and gardens? And so on for ever? And every family in the neighbourhood, every family in the district, every family in the town had two or three girls. Some had four, some had five. One mother had six daughters without a single son, another had seven and one son, and even he seemed predestined to be useless.

So all these parents, these couples, these widows, faced the absolute necessity, the implacable need, to marry off all those daughters, including the five and the six and the seven. And to give them all dowries. Every poor family and every widowed mother with half an acre of land, with a poor little house, was living in misery, and going out to do extra work.

20

They were labouring for families of greater means in their fields, growing figs or mulberries, collecting greenery, producing a little silk. Or else they were looking after two or three ewes or nanny-goats, losing their reputation with the neighbours, paying fines for petty trespass, being mercilessly taxed, eating barley bread watered with bitter sweat. They must, they absolutely must, 'set up' all those daughters, and give them their five, or their six or their seven dowries!

O my God!

And what dowries, by the customs of the islands! 'A house at Kotronia, a vineyard at Ammoudia, an olive grove at Lehouni, a field at Strophlia.' In the last few years, around the mid-century, another burden had been added: the money-count, that which at Constantinople was called dust in the eye, a custom which, unless I am mistaken, the Orthodox Church had forbidden absolutely. Everyone had to give in addition a dowry counted in money. It might be two thousand, or a thousand, or five hundred. Otherwise, he could keep his daughters and enjoy them. He could put them on the shelf. He could shut them up in the cupboard. He could send them to the Museum.

4

That was as far as the sleepless old woman's remembrances and deductions had proceeded. The cock crowed for the second time. It must have been two hours after midnight. The month of January. Night time. North wind blowing. The fire in the hearth was going out. Frankojannou felt a shiver down her back, and her feet were freezing. She wanted to get up and bring in a few sticks from the porch outside, to fling them on the hearth and relight the fire. But she was slow-moving, she felt a stupor, maybe the first sign of the sleep that was overwhelming her.

At that untimely moment, while she still had her eyes shut, there came an unexpected noise outside the door. The old woman woke with a shock. She did not want to shout, 'Who's there?' which would waken the young mother, so she shook off her stupor, broken anyway by the noise of the door. She rose quietly and went out of the room. Before she got to the outer door she heard a discreet, whispering voice.

'Mother!'

She recognized the voice of Amersa, her second daughter.

'What's the matter, dear? What's come over you, at this hour?'

And she opened the door.

'Mother,' continued Amersa with a trembling voice 'How is the poor girl? She isn't dead?'

'No, she's asleep. Now you be quiet,' said the old woman. 'Whatever has come over you?'

'I saw in a dream that she died,' said the tall old maid, with a voice that was still shaking.

'And if she had died, then what?' said the old woman cynically. 'So you got up, and came to see?'

Frankojannou's house — where she usually slept with her two unmarried daughters, though for the time being she spent her nights with the mother of the new baby — was twenty or thirty steps away to the north. The house she was in was Delcharo's, it was part of her dowry, though it was the same old house that Hadoula had built by her thrift, and out of that first nest-egg which she had taken from the hoard of her parents of blessed memory. Later, a few years after Delcharo's marriage, her mother had succeeded in obtaining a second nest as well, smaller and more miserable than the first and situated in the same district. Two or three houses separated one from the other.

It was from that newly built house that Amersa had come at this unauspicious time; she was not afraid of ghosts in the night, she was a bold and resolute girl.

'And so you got up, and came to see?'

'I had a shock in my sleep, Mother. I saw the poor girl was dead, and you had a black cloth in your hand.'

'A black cloth?'

'You were going to wind her up in it. And just as you wound her in the black cloth, your hand went black. And you put your hand in the fire to get rid of the black.'

'Bah! Second-sighted!' said old Hadoula. 'And you made a fool of yourself and came here at this hour . . .'

'I couldn't rest, Mother.'

'And didn't Krinio notice when you left?'

'No, she's asleep.'

'And if she wakes and finds you missing from beside her, what will she think? Won't she shriek out? She'll go mad, the poor girl.'

At present the two sisters slept alone in the little house. Amersa was fearless and inspired confidence, as if she were a man. Their father had died long ago, and the surviving sons were absent overseas.

'I'll go back, Mother,' said Amersa. 'It didn't occur to me that Krinio could wake up at this hour, and be frightened if I wasn't there.'

'You could stay here,' said her mother. 'But what if Krinio wakes up suddenly and takes fright.'

Amersa hesitated for a second.

'Mother,' she said, 'do you want me to stay here, and you go to the house? So that you get some rest, get some peace?'

'No,' replied the old woman, after a moment of thought. 'Now this night's over. It's passed as the others did. To-morrow evening I shall go home, and you can stay here. Only now go along. And good daybreak.'

This whole conversation took place on a narrow porch, just opposite the room where the resonant, many-toned snores of Konstantis could be heard. Amersa, who had arrived barefoot, with the lightest of footsteps, went out, and her mother locked the door from inside.

Amersa went away running. How could she be frightened of ghosts, when she was not afraid of her own brother Mitro, commonly called Moron, or Mulberry or Mug. That scoundrel was the third son of his mother, who used to call him the Saracen dog. He was three years older than Amersa and he had already knifed her once. She saved him, and didn't want to hand him over to the authorities, but he would certainly have knifed her a second time, if he had remained at liberty. Fortunately, he had carried out his murderous attacks elsewhere as well, and in the course of time he got himself shut away in the Venetian dungeons of the old castle at Chalkis.

This is how it happened. Moron or Mulberry was naturally aggressive and wild, even though he had a clever and womanish mind — as his mother used to say, a mind of her making. As a child he taught himself to make beautiful little things: little boats and masks and statues and dolls and so on.

24

He was the neighbourhood scoundrel, flag-bearer of all the villains, and he had at his command all the streetboys, all the barefoot urchins of the roads. He had begun on drunkenness and debauch early in life; he and his little friends organized violent games, riots, childish mob action; he provoked quarrels in the street, he threw stones at all the old men and old women he encountered, and also at the poor and disabled. He left virtually no one undisturbed.

By watching an itinerant knife-maker, he had learnt the trade. He tried, however imperfectly, to make knives. He had a big wheel in the yard, under cover of the balcony, and he had the cellar of the house more or less transformed into a workshop. He ground all the knives and razors of the street-boys, and when he had no more to grind, he ground his own dagger. He had the vanity to make it two-edged, though that was not its original shape. Then he tried making handguns, pistols, tiny cannon, and other instruments of death. All the money he made from dolls, statues and masks, which he didn't drink away, was spent on gunpowder. And he had even attempted to manufacture some himself. Around Easter, and even for two weeks after that, the Mug maintained a rule of terror in his neighbourhood. No one passed by without fear and trembling. The pistol shots were uninterrupted.

One Sunday, the drunken Mulberry created havoc in the road. Two policemen, who had heard numerous complaints about him, were on their way to arrest him and put him 'inside', or 'in Kazarma'. But the Moron was extremely agile and got away. He turned and thumbed his nose from a distance, then he was off once more. He hid in an un-approachable spot in the covered yard of a boat-builder who was his cousin. When the two policemen had given up the pursuit, he summoned the courage to come out into the road.

On that day this same Moron, who had not yet sobered up, chased his own mother down the street, threatening to cut her throat. He complained the old woman had stolen money out of his pocket. He caught her in the yard of the house, where she was running to hide. He pulled her by the hair and dragged her fifty paces along the road.

She yelled out, of course, and neighbours gathered. It was evening, a little before sunset. At the shouting of the neighbours, the two policemen arrived. They had only pretended to give up the chase; in fact they were enraged with this disturber of the peace. As soon as he saw them, Mulberry let his mother go, turned and ran. He had no choice but to hide in the house, since he was in a tight spot, and saw no other refuge nearby that was any safer.

As soon as the old woman, disfigured and covered in dirt, got to her feet, she saw the police and began to beseech them.

'Leave him alone, lads. He's mad, it isn't anything. Don't kill him, lads, with your whips.'

She said this because she saw one of the furious policemen holding a frightening whip in his hand. The two men paid no attention to her entreaties. They went running off in pursuit of the Moron. They broke into his refuge, the cellar where the Moron had his workshop. He had run there to hide, and had just had time to barricade the door. But the panel was rotten and badly fitted, and the Moron had not loved the arts of peace enough to think of mending it. They broke the little barrier and entered. Quick as a weasel, he leapt up and made for the trapdoor to the ground floor. This trapdoor in the ceiling was close to the north wall, which was partly natural rock, and the natural rock offered footholds to the Moron's quick feet. He himself from time to time had cut still more footholds which fitted his feet alone. It seems he often practised this kind of gymnastics.

The trapdoor was shut. The Moron opened it with a butt of his head and a push of his left arm. Then, like a diver surfacing from a wave, he leapt up onto the floor, shut the trapdoor with a bang, and placed some kind of weight, perhaps a small chest, over the wooden panel.

Angry and cursing, the two policemen began to search the lower level. They possessed themselves of all the handguns and knives they found there, also of the wheel and two small anvils, and made ready to leave, or maybe to climb up into the house.

The Mug or Mulberry on the floor above was enraged, drunk still and foaming at the mouth. He was whistling crazily, furiously. His sister Amersa, then a girl of seventeen, had been there alone. She trembled as she saw him fling himself up through the trapdoor in such a mad way. She had heard the footsteps and blasphemies of the two policemen below. She bent down at a little hole between two ill-fitted planks of the floor — or where there was a knot in the wood, gaping and hollow — and by the light from the open cellar window, she saw the two officials.

'Baby, I'll eat you! I'll drink your blood!' growled the Mug. Having nowhere else to vent his rage, he now threatened his sister without cause.

'Quiet! Quiet!' whispered Amersa. 'Oh! Oh dear! My God! Two 'regulars'! Down in the cellar. They're searching. Searching. What are they looking for?'

She saw the two policemen gathering up the little unpolished weapons her brother had made, and the wheel and the anvils. Then suddenly she saw them bent over in a corner, where her mother's weaving loom stood, and she saw one policeman pick up the shuttle. It might have looked like another weapon to him since it is indeed called a weaver's arrow. The other one tried to break off the big cylindrical stone where the newly woven cloth was wound away. Perhaps he had never seen anything like it in his life and imagined it too would do very nicely as a weapon.

When Amersa saw this, she uttered a strangled cry. She wanted to yell out to them to leave the stone and the arrow, but the sound died away in her mouth.

'Shut up, baby,' grunted Mulberry. 'What are you up to? What are you laughing at?'

Mulberry in his drunkenness had taken that inarticulate cry of his sister's for laughter.

A few minutes later the two policemen went outside. They had glanced at the trapdoor, which they had seen close just as they entered the cellar. Amersa got to her feet. She seemed to hear a squeak on the lowest tread of the outside stairs which were wooden and covered by the broad balcony. She ran to the door.

She imagined that the two 'regulars', as she called them, were climbing the steps, and perhaps breaking open the door of the house. She bent at the key-hole, trying to see and understand what was going on through the tiny hole. The only window with a view was shuttered and she had no other means of seeing out.

The Moron, when he saw Amersa run to the door, imagined, in his drunken confusion, that his sister wanted to open the door and hand him over to the police. Blind with rage, he drew out a sharpened knife from behind his waist, and leapt and stabbed his sister in the back, under the right shoulder-blade.

At the touch of the cold steel, Amersa let out a terrible shriek.

The two policemen had not yet gone away, they were stationed close by the cellar door, and discussing what action to take. When they heard that shriek of terror, they looked up and came running.

They clattered up the stairs and reached the balcony. They shook the door violently.

'In the name of the Law! Open up!'

At that moment the suspicion came to one of the police-men that the wanted man might be able to escape by way of the trapdoor and the cellar. He turned to the other policeman and said,

'Mind he doesn't get away down the chute, through that trapdoor. God knows where we'll have to look for him then!'

'What do you mean?' said the other, not understanding at once.

'What I'm telling you!' went on the first. 'Do what I'm busting myself telling you!'

The second policeman, for all his apparent stupidity, ran down as fast as he could to shut the cellar door, or else to guard it. But he was already too late. The Moron had dragged aside the little chest, got the trap open, and jumped down. It was a drop of more than six foot, but he was light and agile. The floor below was strewn with axes and saws, yet he landed safely and on his feet.

Running like the wind, he knocked over the policeman, who fell heavily at the foot of the outer stairs. Mulberry was off, like lightning. He ran off up to Kotronia where the owls live. It was a rocky hill towering up over the back of the house, where Mulberry knew all the hide-outs. No policeman or anyone else had ever managed to catch him up there.

But just as Mulberry had been at the point of jumping down through the trapdoor, he remembered for some reason — maybe because he was already sobered by events or had 'sweated it out' as he would have said — he remembered that after he had knifed his sister the knife had fallen from his hand and lay on the floor. Maybe he had dropped it because fear and remorse had come on him at that moment, and maybe for that same reason he had cut his sister's body only superficially with the blade.

Because he knew the police were not rushing to the living quarters, he had no time to go back to the door, bend down and pick up the knife, so just as he was about to jump he shouted to his sister:

'The strife, baby! See and hide that strife!'

He chose that expression, so that the police would not hear the word knife. Already a wanted criminal, he invoked the

29

affection of his sister to save him in that fearful moment. It was the measure of his confidence in her. The knife would be bloody, and his pursuers would see the blood. Begging that the instrument be hidden, he was hoping his crime would be too.

And in fact Amersa bent down and picked up the knife. The blood was already running from her wound. She could see that the door, which was made of thin old planks with rotten nails and hinges, would certainly be broken down. She was already close to losing consciousness. But she did it. Then she dragged herself to the corner where there was a little divan: a pile of folded sheets, pillows and blankets.

She hid the bloody knife under the whole heap, wrapped herself in an old, worn but clean coverlet and sat down on the low pile, which sank lower under her weight. She put her left hand to her shoulder and tried to stop the blood. Strangely, she was not frightened when she saw her own blood, even though it was for the first time. The whole thing was like a dream to her. She just gritted her teeth and wondered why she felt no pain yet. Then after a few minutes she did feel a sharp stab.

At the same moment, the door sank inwards. One of the policemen jumped noisily into the house.

Amersa did not raise her head, she was hunched and wrapped up to the nose in her coverlet.

'Where is he, the villain?' roared the policeman.

Amersa gave no answer.

The soldier had not noticed the Moron's escape, nor the fall of his own comrade, maybe because that moment coincided exactly with his forcing of the door, and the one noise drowned and smothered the other. He searched the whole of the hall where Amersa was, then ran into the winter living-room and then the bedroom. He found no one. Only the trapdoor was open.

A moment later the other policeman arrived upstairs.

30

'He got off?'

'Got down that trap.'

'And you were cheering? You didn't stop him?'

'I got it on the head. Ach, what a getaway. Seven sea-miles an hour.'

'Ah,' said the first policeman, shaking his head violently and bending the index finger of his right hand, and bringing it to his mouth as if to bite it. 'Just what we needed to get ourselves demoted.'

The second policeman, wanting to play the official, turned to the young woman.

'Where's your brother gone off to, child?' he asked her.

Amersa gave no answer. Except that maybe she whispered inside herself with unwilling irony, and with all the dreadful pain and anguish that she felt: 'You know where.'

'Why are you sitting there, girl?' asked the first policeman more kindly. 'Has anything happened to you?'

Amersa shook her head.

'What did he want with you? Did he go to knife you?'

'Why did you yell out?' added the second one.

Amersa answered the first policeman's question.

'No!'

'Truly, he didn't knife you?' the man insisted.

Amersa replied with natural insistence.

'My brother! For him to knife me!'

'Why are you sitting there? What's the matter? Are you ill?'

'I have fever.'

Amersa had not considered that the floor or even the straw might have been stained with blood. The sun had already set and it was dusk inside the house. The place where the bloody knife had fallen lay in shadow, behind the half-door, two thirds open and nearly touching the wall, so that the two men did not see the red stains.

'Why did you yell out?' the first policeman insisted.

31

'I had a pain and I was dizzy,' said Amersa.

And at that very moment, as if to confirm her words, she really did faint. She cried out Oh! through gritted teeth, and fell forwards. The two officials were disturbed, they looked at one another, and the first said,

'But where's her mother?'

As if in response to this call, Frankojannou came running.

'It's the old woman the boy was dragging along by the hair, right in the shit,' said the second policeman.

Then he added:

'Won't you tell me, old lady, where your son's got to?'

Frankojannou did not answer. She ran to Amersa. She was an adaptable healer and she was capable of looking after her daughter.

All this came back to Amersa's memory again and again in the long hours of the night, from sunset to dawn, as she lay sleepless in the little house beside her young sister, sleeping Krinio; just as night after night their mother Hadoula lay sleepless in her elder daughter's house not far away. When Amersa got home to the little house after her night-time expedition, undertaken because of her second-sight, and because of her dream, she saw by the dim light of the lamp that burnt before the small, ancient, blackened ikon of the Virgin, that her younger sister Krinio was still asleep. She did not look as if she had so much as stirred in her sleep. Only as Amersa came in did Krinio, as if she had heard the slight creaking dimly through her sleep, shift peacefully; she sighed and turned over without waking.

Second-sighted in reality! The words her mother had just used came back to her as she was going home to her sister after the third cock-crow. But was she genuinely second-sighted? She whose dreams and delusions and imaginings had often foretold something, or revealed something, or left some strange impression. Even her lies when she told them became the truth against her will. As when she was answering the police questions after that knifing she had had from her brother. When she said, 'I had a pain. I was dizzy!', a real fainting fit came over her, as if some higher, daemonic will wanted to cover up her lie.

Amersa went back to bed beside her sister, but she was restless. Memories continued to revisit her, intense but less overwhelming and less dark-winged than her mother's. And for those long hours, she never ceased to mull over the fate of her brother, the Moron, who was in prison now in Chalkis.

5

When Amersa had gone, Frankojannou, who was crouching
in the corner between hearth and cradle, lost touch with sleep
once again. Bitter wandering thoughts reinvaded her. When
her two elder sons had gone overseas to America and Delcharo
had grown up, it was time for her to act effectively on her
daughter's behalf. All the world knows what it means for a
woman, not yet widowed, to be both mother and father to her
daughters. She has to marry them off and endow them and be
matchmaker and negotiator as well. She has to give house and
vineyard, field and olive trees. Like a man, she has to borrow
money, she has to run to the notary, she has to mortgage her
property. As a woman, she also has to provide or procure a
dowry, that is a trousseau, sheets, embroidered blouses, silk
clothing hemmed with gold thread. As a matchmaker, she
has to hunt down a son-in-law, pursue him, net him, and
bring him in alive. And what a son-in-law!

One like Konstantis, who was snoring now, beyond the
partition, in the next bedroom. He was an ill-made, bald-
headed fellow who looked like nothing on earth. And at that,
he had his caprices and his demands and his eccentricities.
Today he wanted one thing, tomorrow another: one day so
much, and the next day a lot more. Before the match, he had
often listened to mean and envious people, paid heed to
slander from this direction and that, involved himself in slick
intrigues, and just not wanted to get settled. And then just
after the engagement he installed himself in his mother-in-
law's house, and put an early one in the oven all of a sudden.

And all the time it had to be 'Yes sir, No sir'.

And then in the end, after an age of ten thousand troubles and anguish inexpressible, to be able to persuade a son-in-law like that to come to the altar! And the bride peacocking in precious clothes, the fruit of years of thrift and fasting, a bride with no waist to set off the lithe little figure she used to have.

And three months after the wedding for her to produce a daughter, and a son after three more years, and another daughter after another two, this new-born baby, for the sake of which old granny had been sleepless so many nights.

And for each of those daughters, the mother was going to suffer as much, and as much again, and as much yet again, as her own mother had suffered on her account.

And the unhappy manwoman Amersa was still unmarried, may her prayer be answered. She had the luck. A sensible girl. What joy would she have got from the agonies of this world? And she wasn't even envious! Envy what? She looked at her elder sister and she was sorry for her. It made her heart bleed.

As for Krinio, the little one, if only God would give her the grace! However things might be, her mother had no intention (she couldn't manage any more, couldn't cope) of putting up with a tiny fraction of what she had suffered for her sister, just in order to marry her off. But I ask you, do there really have to be so many daughters? And if so, is it worth the trouble of bringing them up? 'Isn't there,' asked Frankojannou, 'isn't there always death and always a cliff?' Better for them to make haste above. 'You're telling me, neighbour.'

The suffering woman felt a great and holy relief, when it happened that in the little procession led by the priest and the Cross, it was she who followed behind, bearing in compassion and sympathy the little coffin shaped like a cradle. It was the funeral procession of a neighbour's or a distant relative's little daughter. She was unable to understand what the priest was murmuring as he nibbled away the words between his teeth. 'There is nothing more compassionate than the father, nothing more unhappy than the mother. For often before the tomb they beat their breasts and say, 'O my son, my sweetest child, hearest thou not thy mother's voice? Behold the belly that bore thee. Why doest thou not speak as thou hast spoken unto us: Alleluiah!' And again, 'O child, who is there that shall not lament, beholding thine appearance, thy withered face, which was delightful as the rose'.''

She was enormously pleased when ten minutes walk brought the little procession to the Tombs. Beautiful country, everlasting spring, blossom time, wild flowers, murmur of cultivated ground! Behold the garden of the dead! O, Paradise, already out of this world, was opening its gates to receive this innocent little creature, which had the good fortune to relieve its parents of so many sufferings. Hail ye little angels flitting round and round on wings all gold and white, and ye souls of the Saints receive it!

When she returned to the house of death to attend the ceremony of consolation in the evening, old Hadoula could find no word of comfort to say. She was all joy and she blessed the innocent child and its parents. And grief was joy and death was life and everything was upside down.

Ah, look . . . Nothing is exactly what it seems, anything but, in fact rather the opposite. Given that grief is joy and death is life and resurrection, then disaster is happiness and disease is health. So are all those scourges that seem so ugly, that mow down ungrown infants, the smallpox and scarlet fever and diphtheria and the rest of the diseases, are they not really happiness? Loving gestures and wingbeats of the little angels who rejoice in the heavens when they receive the souls of children? And we humans in our blindness think of these things as unhappy, as the strokes of heaven, as an evil thing.

And the poor parents lose their wits, and pay so much for

quacks and threepenny drugs, to save their child. They never suspect that when they think of saving, they are really losing their offspring. And Christ had said, as Frankojannou had heard her confessor explain, that he that loves his soul shall lose it, and he that hates his own soul shall keep it unto life everlasting.

Would it not really be right, if only humans were not so blind, to assist the scourge that fluttered in the angels' wings, instead of trying to pray it away? But look, the little angels take no sides and make no favours. They take away boys and girls alike into Paradise. In fact all the more boys. So many precious only sons who died untimely.

Girls have seven lives, the old woman reflected. Not much makes them ill and they seldom die. Should we as good Christians not help in the work of the angels? Oh how many boys, and how many little princes are snatched away untimely! And even little princesses die more easily, rare in their sex as they are, more easily than the infinite multitude of female children of the poor. The only ones with seven lives are the girl children of the lowest class! They seem to have been multiplied on purpose, to punish their parents with a foretaste of hell in this world. Ah, the more one works things out, the more one's brain goes up like smoke.

At that moment the little girl began to cough and cry. Having worked out so many high matters, and deeply excited by the sea-waves of her memories, the old woman suddenly felt dizzy with the sea-rocking and the stormy passage of her lifetime. She began to lose consciousness, she drowsed uncontrollably.

The little child coughed and cried and fussed 'like a grown up person'. Its grandmother shifted, turned, and woke again.

The mother slept deeply on without hearing cough or cry.

The old woman opened her bleary eyes, and made an impatient, threatening gesture.

'Eh, shut up will you?' she said.

37

Frankojannou's brain really had begun to smoke. She had gone out of her mind in the end. It was the consequence of her proceeding to high matters. She leant over the cradle. She pushed two long, tough fingers into the baby's mouth to shut it up.

She knew it was not all that usual for very small children to shut up. But she was now out of her mind. She did not know very clearly what she was doing, nor did she admit to herself what she wanted to do.

She kept her fingers there for a long time. Then she withdrew them from the little mouth, which had ceased to breathe, and pulled at the baby's throat, and squeezed it for a few minutes.

That was all.

Frankojannou failed to recollect her daughter's dream, though she had been told it only an hour ago, between the second and the third crowing of the cock.

Her brain had gone up in smoke.

6

Once Amersa had broken her sleep, and then come home again from the house of child-birth, she lay without sleeping by the side of her younger sister, and went on thinking about her brother, the unhappy criminal. From the moment when he jumped through the trapdoor and ran away, she had never seen him again. The police kept after him for days, but they never found him.

Immediately after the police questioning, to which Amersa gave the answers we have recorded, her mother reached the house. She found her wrapped in the coverlet, head fallen forward, very pale from the fainting fit which had followed her loss of blood.

To the question of one of the policemen, the one the Moron had knocked over as he fled, 'Old woman, where is your son?' Frankojannou had not replied. But the other one, who seemed more human, said gently:

'See what's the matter with your daughter, Mam. Says she's ill.'

'Ill! Of course she's ill!' replied Frankojannou readily. 'She's been terrified by the doings of my cursed son. Look, lads. If you do catch him, don't be too terrible to him.'

'Did you see where he ran? Where was he making for?'

'I saw him from a distance. He was making for the walls, away over at the threshing floors.'

Frankojannou was a double liar. She had not seen him, but she was certain he would have headed in the opposite direction from the one she said, towards Kotronia, above the

39

house to the east where he'd hunted owls as a little boy.

The two men went off at a trot. One of them as he went threw a last suspicious glance through the half open door.

Hadoula shut the door, but at the same time she opened the window.

'He knifed me mother,' groaned Amersa painfully, recovering from her faint as she felt the draught of fresh air that came through the open window beside her. She flung off the coverlet, and the blood showed on the jersey she wore over her undershirt.

'Oagh! Aagh! The murderer! May God and the earth have him!' cursed her mother as she saw the blood.

And she began to stroke her daughter, and to try to stop the blood, and to bind up the wound. She took off the jersey, pulled off the sleeve of the undershirt, and bared Amersa's right arm, which was pale and scraggy, but strong and muscular all the same.

The wound was superficial, but nonetheless the blood was flowing. Hadoula used whatever salve she knew, maybe a 'bloodstopper' if she had one, and she tied up the wound. The blood soon ceased.

Amersa had suffered a shock, but she was strong, courageous and without fear. In fact, in a few days, thanks to her mother's care, the wound had healed.

Frankojannou would never have called in the doctor. She did not want it known that her son had knifed his sister. To all those well-wishers among the neighbours who questioned her, sometimes she denied with affected anger, sometimes with a forced laugh, but always she denied that the Mulberry had wounded her daughter. Her great interest was to find out whether he had escaped the hands of the police. After that it was up to the mercy of God.

In fact she had news after a few days that her son had gone away to sea, taking ship as a sailor secretly and at night. He had escaped from the island. The harbour master's secretary was an accommodating, helpful man who had no hesitation in enrolling him as a sailor. Mulberry was hardly twenty then, and Amersa was just seventeen.

Time went by before the family heard any more of the fugitive. Finally, after a year and more, there was an indefinite rumour of his committing a murder on board the ship he sailed in. When his sisters heard that, they told the world they knew nothing about it, and prayed with all their hearts that the rumour might be false. But his mother in her heart of hearts believed that the news was true.

A few days later they got a letter with the postal stamp of Chalkis. He was writing from the prison of that city. Putting the last things first, he made a song and dance about his tortures and sufferings in the dungeons of the Venetian castle. Then with a penitent heart, but in double meanings and as it were between the lines, he admitted that he might really have murdered the man, old Portaitis, the ship's quartermaster, only without knowing what he was doing, and without really intending it. (In fact, he would genuinely not have wished to have murdered him.) The devil had possessed him, it was not his fault at all, the murder was in the heat of a quarrel. His soul had been disturbed. It had been proved that the knife 'belonged to the victim'. Maybe he had snatched it, he could not remember how, out of the body of the murdered man. He was inclined to believe he had taken it from the man's hand.

Then he went back to his own sufferings, these last two months in prison. He proceeded to call upon the affection of his mother, and to persuade her to arise, without fail, and go to seek out the widow of Portraitis, the murdered man, and also his daughter, to beseech them with tears, to achieve the impossible, to get them to beg for the murderer's release!

'Rise up, mother, and take ship, go over to Platana·and speak to Portaitina, and also her daughter Karikleia, and get them to beg for me to go free, and I will be a son to them, and

41

take Karikleia for my wife without a dowry, and we shall all lead a good and loving life. And let them see how I will love Karikleia and how I'll take the old one for my mother-in-law, and work like a slave to keep them, with many good things, because I can be trusted and I know how to make money.' The murderer went on to refer for the third time to his sufferings and promised that as soon as he was out of prison he would bring many beautiful objects and adornments as dowries for his two sisters, and dolls and toys as well for the children of his elder sister Delcharo.

It is no wonder, really, that Frankojannou did not hesitate. She borrowed a little money on security of all her silver, took ship, and crossed over to the opposite island, to the village of Platana, where she went and sought out the widow of Portaitis. What is strange is that with her flattering facility of tongue, her womanly cunning and the thousands of lies she knew how to tell — she was fifty-five at that time, but still lively and in full womanly bloom — Frankojannou succeeded in persuading the murdered man's old widow. Mother and daughter even gave hospitality to the mother of the murderer. Frankojannou, paying the expense of the journey herself, persuaded her, as I said, to go off with her to Chalkis. Together they would plead with the Magistracy, the Court and the jury, for the release or the acquital of the accused. As for the daughter, Karikleia, she stated that she sought no revenge, since it would not bring her father back. But she would never want to have the murderer as her husband, she would prefer to remain unmarried for ever and ever.

The two old women went together to Chalkis and stayed
'there for three months. They lived in a hovel in the ruins of a Turkish house, near the Jewish quarter, by the upper gate of the Castle. And every day Hadoula went to the prison in the morning as the prisoners came out. She was usually accompanied by Portaitis' widow, who sat with her back to the prison and waited, being unwilling to see the face of the

42

murderer. Coming out from the big, shabby old church of Hayia Paraskevi, they made their sign of the cross, and the mother brought the accused sesame bread, figs, sardines, and tobacco for his pipe. And hidden in the deep pocket of her skirt she kept in store a little bottle of rum or raki, for his consolation in prison.

Two or three times a week they came out through the Upper Gate of the castle, and saw hanging there, in the dark gateway, the leg-bone of 'the Greek giant' and his slipper of monstrous size. The two of them stored up such sights for whenever by good luck they should get back to their villages, to tell their grandchildren what they had seen. Then they cut straight down through the district of Souvala, or by Saint Dimitrios, and visited the Magistrate, whose clerk got rid of them, and the judges, who sometimes consented to laugh with them.

When in the end the trial was definitely announced, they tried to get close to the jury, some of them in kilts from mountain villages, others in breeches from the islands and the coast. Frankojannou promised all of them presents of a thousand kinds, and she would have been capable of fulfilling her promises too, if she had possessed scented wines, and fine amber-coloured oil, and lobster-tails, and carp paté, and red caviar, and dried octopus, and the best figs and everything else that her island produced.

She promised one of the jurors, who was yellow-faced and coughing and appeared to be in pain, that she could cure him with an ointment she knew. But all she could do was not enough, and the murderer was condemned to twenty years in prison. Her plans suffered the same shipwreck as the family alliance which might have linked murderer's mother and victim's widow.

Now they had to return home, but their little money was exhausted, all they had brought with them, and all that Amersa had managed to send them meanwhile by going out

43

to work and by sewing at home.

In vain Frankojannou implored every ship she saw ready to sail for the Gulf of Histiaia at least to take Portaitis' widow, who was older and weaker. For herself she had her own plan, and when she saw that the captains were demanding not only a fare, but that the traveller must bring food, and that if they left her at Stylis or Oreoi, she would still have to find a boat to her own village, she told the secret of her plan to Portaitaina.

'I,' she said, 'am capable of walking with my two feet from here to Saint Anna on dry land, they say it's two days' journey, and there we shall find the mailship, our own Captain Petserelos who knows us, the mail captain, and he'll take us. I'll save up my expenses on the journey by gathering plants and weeds and wild greens, and any Christian woman I find with a sick child or a sick husband, I'll do false cures to help him, and put her under an obligation. Can you manage? Are your ankles up to it?'

'What else am I to do? Whether I can or I can't,' replied Portaitaina. 'Better we go together as we came.'

And they set out. Hadoula did as she had said, except that they lingered rather on the road because the widow's pace was slow. But she was successful beyond her hopes. When at the end of a week she reached home, she had something over from the enterprise. Her activities brought her a bag of wheat, about a pound of cheese, two birds, a woollen scarf she got as a present, and a few drachmas in ready money. From this she generously paid Portaitaina's fare as well, to get her home to her own fireside.

Amersa remembered it all very well, since her mother had never stopped talking about it ever since. Twelve years had gone by now, her brother was still in prison, her father had died long ago, Statharos and Yalis had never come back from America, and little Giorgakis had taken to the high seas in his turn. Krinio had grown up, Delcharo had had another girl, and Amersa herself had remained an old maid.

7

——◆——

After the cough and cry of the little girl had so suddenly been
cut off, complete silence, peace prevailed in the dark bedroom, Frankojannou had bent her head. She supported her
forehead with both hands and ceased to think. She did not
feel she was alive any longer. Not even her breathing could be
heard. Every noise had ceased. No flame crackled on the
hearth, not a sound was heard, and the half-burnt wick of the
lamp shone painfully. The tiny votive flame before the ikons
had gone out long ago, and the forms of the saints could be
seen no longer.

Suddenly the mother woke with a shock into complete
quiet.

'What is it, mother?' she said.

Her mother regarded her dazedly and deludedly in the
light of the lamp.

'What is it? Nothing!' she said. 'Did you wake?'

'I thought you said something. Cried out to me in my
sleep.'

'Me? No. It was inside your head.'

'What time is it, mother?'

'What time? How should I know?' So many times the bird
had spoken and spoken.

'Haven't you been to sleep, mother?'

'I had a good bellyful of sleep. Wore away my ribs,' said
Frankojannou, who had not shut her eyes. 'It's close to dawn.'

The new mother yawned, and made the sign of the cross
over her mouth. At the same time she raised her glance to the

45

little group of ikons, which she noticed.

'The flame has gone out, mother, did you not light it?'

'I never noticed it, daughter,' said the old woman. 'I was deep asleep.'

'I see the baby's sleeping quietly as well. How did she manage it?'

'She's gone to sleep at last,' said the old woman.

'And my breast hurts,' said the mother. 'It's begun to make a lot of milk now. I wish she was awake and I could give her the breast.'

'Eh, what's to be done. We'll find a child,' said the old woman.

'What are you saying, mother?'

The old woman gave no answer. She wanted to say something. She did not know what to say.

'Won't you take the trouble to light the flame, mother?'

'If you want it, you get up and light it. I have no hands.'

'What?'

'My poor hand's paralysed.'

'What are you saying? Be sensible, mother. How can I light the flame when I haven't been to church?'

At that moment, as she said 'my hand's paralysed', Amersa's dream rose up in the old woman's head for the first time.

She could not control herself, and she stifled a deep groan in her breast.

What's the matter, mother?'

The mother jumped out of her low bed.

'Is the child not well?'

Screams, convulsions, cries were heard. The mother had found her little daughter dead in the cradle.

Konstantis in the next room, who had slept his fill, woke at the noise.

'What is it?' he roared, rubbing his eyes.

He yawned and stretched and leapt up and ran to the

bedroom door.

'Here, what are you up to? You'll get all the world up on its feet. Couldn't you allow us at least to get a bit of sleep, with your screaming?'

No one replied to Konstantis' protests. His wife was bending over the cradle, stifling her sobs. His mother-in-law was sitting with her hands clasped, enigmatic, gritting her teeth, a fixed expression on her face. After the first stifled groan, she had uttered no further sound.

'What! The child's dead? Here!' said Konstantis, and his mouth hung open.

Then he added:

'This is why I had some upside down dreams. Oh the devil!'

Delcharo turned from the cradle for a moment, still sobbing, and said:

'Mother, won't you bring its little clothes, and we'll change it? Where's Amersa?

Frankojannou did not answer.

'Where's Amersa, mother?' went on Delcharo, touching her mother on the arm.

Frankojannou shook as if she had been pricked with a thorn or stung.

'Where's Amersa? At home,' she answered.

'Didn't Amersa come here? I thought I heard her voice through my sleep,' said the young mother.

'Let him go and call her,' said the old woman, gesturing with a flicker of her eye towards her son-in-law.

'Konstantis, will you go and call Amersa?' said the young mother to her husband.

'I'm going. That's it then. Ach, what a pity. Oh the devil. Just as well we baptized it, anyway.'

He bent to the floor of the little entrance in the darkness, feeling around for his old shoes to put on. He made a little noise, knocking old pairs of clogs together and banging the wooden floor.

'Where are my old shoes?' he said.

In the end he put on a pair of worn-out women's slippers that covered only the tips of his toes and part of his foot and left his ankles bare. He made more noise opening the door, as he was unable to find the latch or the bolt in the dark. When he had it open he suddenly turned back.

'Listen, Delcharo,' he said, 'shall I just bring Amersa or Krinio as well? What do you think, mother-in-law?'

Frankojannou answered impatiently:

'Get off now, what are you turning back about? Let anyone come who's coming.'

Delcharo wailed quietly bending over the cradle.

Konstantis, before he left, threw a glance at the cradle and at his wife.

'Ach, what a pity, curse it,' he said. 'And I saw some dreams! Oh my goodness!'

And he set off running.

8

One morning in Holy Week Frankojannou went off on her own into the country to Mammo's brook. She wanted to pay a visit to the little olive grove she had got as a death-present from a God-relation of hers who was quite well off. He had died without heirs and she had done him services. She had given half of these trees to Delcharo for her dowry, but the other half were still her own.

A few weeks had gone by since the events we have related. There had been no particular commotion about the little daughter of Delcharo Trachilaina, they buried her the same day. Even if she noticed certain black marks round the little child's throat, the baby's mother would never have dared to speak about them, nor would anyone have believed the charge against her own mother. Obviously the child had died of fever.

The only doctor there had ever been in the village for years, kindly Dr B the Bavarian, happened to be away. There was a rumour of cholera in Egypt and the Home Office preferred to send this particular doctor to look after the isolation hospital on Delos.

The government had sent in his place as temporary health officer an aged doctor, Dr M, who had not yet arrived. In the meanwhile there was an ex-medical student living on the island. He was called in by the local police to verify the death. He took a superficial look at the dead infant's face and complained of not being called while it was alive. Then he filled in a certificate that named 'death from convulsive coughing'.

From that day onwards old Hadoula lived a life of remorse and worry. She looked as if she had put ashes on her grey hair, so motionless and slightly bowed did she hold her head. She wore her long black kerchief as if it was a symbol of penitence. When Lent began, she went to church often, she made numerous deep genuflections, she prepared for confession and put it off. She fasted on dry bread without oil for five days in every week, and observed complete three-day fasts in the first week and at mid-Lent. She was ashamed to look at her daughter Delcharo, and avoided meeting her glance.

That day in Holy Week, Frankojannou had climbed very early in the morning to the crest of a high, rocky hill to the west of the town, where the melancholy observer sees a little cemetery with white tombs spread out below on the high and sea-lashed tongue of land. The eye moves away in search of brightness and life to the peaceful waves, to the broad triple anchorage and the green and charming islets which fence it in from the east and the south. High on that crest, a lonely landmark, glittering in the light of day, stands the chapel of Saint Anthony. Frankojannou came to it and made the sign of the cross, but while she intended to enter, at the last moment she hesitated and continued on her way. 'I am not worthy,' she said inside herself, 'to enter a chapel where they say Mass so often. Better I go to St John in Hiding.'

Later she arrived at the olive grove, and examined each and every tree to see if they were fruiting yet. It was already mid-April! Easter had come late. She prayed inwardly to Christ 'to grant oil unto the poor'. For two years the olive trees had been barren and there were signs of a creeping blight that destroyed the fruit and blackened the branches of the trees.

When she had stayed a short while in the olive grove, she got to her feet and with many backward looks as if she were saying goodbye to the trees she went away. She walked down to the brook and began to climb along its course, as she had done so often before. With her basket on her left arm, and her knife in her right hand, she bent down, in all the places she knew, to find kavkalis and dandelions and chervil and anise to fill her basket. She would make a cake on Holy Saturday and eat it with her daughters, and have some over to give to the neighbours from whom she would not lose in return.

Apart from these weeds, which every woman knew how to find, Hadoula knew other plants useful for curing illnesses, mallow and serpentary and wild onion, growing among the arbutus and the ferns and by the roots of the wild trees, and the mushrooms and thorns and fleabane, and the maidenhair in the little waterfalls of the stream, which they say is a cure for puerperal fever.

When she had collected enough herbs of this medicinal kind, which she wrapped in a separate kerchief inside the basket, the hour was turning to evening and the sun was approaching the crest of the mountain. The shadow was deep in the valley, and the noise of her footsteps resounded like heavy strokes in the depths of her soul.

The old woman climbed higher up to the steep top of the valley. Below her the river cut deep through the Acheilas ravine, and its stream filled all the deep valley with soft murmurs. In appearance it was motionless and lakelike, but in reality perpetually in motion under the tall and long-tressed planes. Among mosses and bushes and ferns it prattled secretly, kissed the trunks of the trees, creeping like a serpent along the length of the valley, green-coloured from leafy reflections, kissing and biting at once at the rocks and the roots, a murmuring, limpid stream, full of little crabs which ran to hide in piles of sand, while a shepherd, letting the little lambs graze on the dewy greenery, came to lean down over the water, and pull out a stone to hunt them with. The talkative, unceasing twitter of thrushes re-echoed in the forest that crowned all the western slopes and crept up the crest of Anagyro to the Eagle's Nest. There it was said that a sea-eagle had nested for three human generations and gone away in the end without leaving any young. In its abandoned nest was found an entire museum of monstrous bones of sea-snakes, seals, dogfish and other marine monsters, which the huge, powerful bird, with its blue hooked beak and its vast cinder-coloured wings, had picked out of the seas in the course of time.

Up on the crest of the gorge, on a shoulder between two mountains, in between the crags of Konomos and Little Anagyro, the ancient and deserted monastery of St John in Hiding survived. It really was in hiding. It lay behind a little neck of ground, sheltered by the two mountains and the dense growth. One approached it either from the north, as Frankojannou now, from the Acheilas gorge, or from the south, from the area called the crags of Konomos, and even if one passed close to the ancient holy place, it wa impossible to suspect its existence unless one knew the lie of the land as well as Frankojannou knew it.

The enclosure and the few cells were all that survived from many more. The chapel was still standing, but it was deserted and Mass was not said in it. The nave still had a roof, but the roof of the sanctuary had fallen in on the north side, and roof-tiles and debris had covered the altar. There was a wooden screen, once carved and gilded, now ruined and unrecognizable, and the ikons were missing. The few wall-paintings had perished from damp and the faces of the Saints could no longer be distinguished.

Only on the right of the choir there remained a wall-painting that represented Saint John the Baptist bearing witness to Christ. 'Behold the Lamb of God who taketh away the sins of the world.' The face and the hand of the Baptist, which was stretched out and pointing, showed up rather well. The Saviour's face was terribly dim on the wet wall.

In the old days St John in Hiding was the shrine of all who

had a secret burden or a hidden sin. Old Hadoula knew that old belief, that old custom, and that was why she had thought of coming today to the ancient and deserted chapel to offer her supplications. She preferred a church where Mass was not said; even at the parish church where she went so often all that Lent, she only dared to go in to the narthex behind one leaf of the women's door, which was shut with a bolt, as if she felt the need to be ready to run away as soon as she was thrown out. She was not so much frightened of Papanikolas, the austere and ascetic parish priest, or Dimitros the warden. Dimitros was always growling and rude to old women who insisted on not going up into the women's part of the church; they held out for their tiny place in the northwest corner, fenced round with stalls and tables. She was not frightened of him; she feared the Archangel with the furious expression, flaming scimitar in his hand, whose tall painting was on the north gate of the church.

She entered the deserted chapel, lit a candle which she had in her basket with a few matches, and made three prostrations before the half ruined wall-painting. Then, turning over in her mind the idea which had obsessed her but which she had never voiced aloud, she spoke in a voice that could have been heard, had there been any witness of that scene: 'If I was right, dear Saint John, send me a sign today, and I'll do a good deed, a Christian good deed, for my soul to be at peace and my poor heart.'

9

She had filled her basket and the sun had sunk very low, when she came out of the deserted chapel. Old Hadoula set out for the town. She made her way down the ravine, turned away to the right and began to climb up to the hill of St Anthony, as she had come. But before she got to the crest of the hill, where the big view opened out on the harbour and the town, she saw on her right low down in the depth of the little valley which is called Mammo's brook, and which meets the deep valley of the Acheilas at an obtuse angle, the broad well-cultivated garden of Iannis Perivolas and she said to herself:

'I'll go to Iannis' bit of ground and ask him if he'll give me a bundle of onions or a lettuce. What have I got to lose?'

At the same time she remembered what she had heard a few days earlier, that the wife of Iannis Perivolas was ill. She had no idea whether the wife was inside the hut by the garden entrance or whether she was laid up in the town. But the gardener himself would certainly be there, she concluded, since she could see from a distance that the garden gate was open. So she considered selling him her services, with the plants she had in her basket, and the promise of 'drugs' to cure his wife. And then she said to herself:

'What services can you do to poor people? The biggest service you could do them would be to have some barrenweed to give them. God forgive me! Or if it was boyweed,' she went on. 'Because she makes so many girls, this poor woman. Five or six so far, I'm sure. I don't know if any have died, any of those seven-lived ones.'

She had in fact searched for many years in the mountains and the ravines to find boyweed for her daughter, but what she had given her had not succeeded. In fact it worked more as girlweed. And yet for herself in the past, when her sister-in-law gave her some, it had accomplished its purpose, and she made four sons and only three daughters. As for the barrenweed, her confessor had told her years ago, it was a terrible sin.

Before she got to the garden gate, as she came down the hillside path, she saw that Iannis Perivolas was not in his garden, but at that moment in the next field, which it seemed he had rented as a tenant from the neighbour. The field was sown with barley, very green and in spike already; it lay at a slightly lower level than the garden, about knee height below it. Iannis was bending over at one edge of the field, and appeared to be herb-gathering or else uprooting some ugly weeds and tares from among the crop while it was still light and the sun was sinking. He was over beyond the other end of the garden, and when Frankojannou approached the garden gate she no longer had him in view. He was hidden by the dense hedge, and far enough away for her to be unable to shout him a Good Evening. He was bent, and quite absorbed in his work; he did not even see her.

Old Hadoula went through. Near the gate was the hut, more or less white, with outside walls not perfectly finished or perfectly clean. It did not seem to have been whitewashed for a long time, and it bore witness to the illness of the lady of the house. In front of it was a disorder of tools, vegetables and bundles. The door was shut. The two windows shut. There was just one glass fanlight, but for Frankojannou to get up there, craning at her full height, to see if there was anyone inside, she would have to climb the two or three steps and reach the little unfenced plankwalk called a 'balcony'.

While she was hesitating whether she ought to do that, or just climb onto the balcony and knock at the door, she heard the voices of little girls. A little further off was the well with the pulley, and next to it the cistern, low-lying and deep, with its sides just appearing above the surface of the ground. On the constructed bank at the lip of the cistern sat two little girls, one about five years old, the other about three, playing with a reed and a string and a hook tied to the end, as if they were fishing in the cistern.

There, Saint John has sent me a sign, said Frankojannou to herself almost involuntarily, as she saw the two girls. What a relief for poor Perivolou, if they fell in the cistern and went swimming! Now let's see, is there any water in it?

She came close and bent over and saw that the cistern was nearly full, two thirds of a fathom of water.

Why does he leave them here, that father of theirs, such little girls? said Frankojannou. Couldn't they fall in quite easily on their own?

She turned an anxious glance to the hut. But she had the impression that there was no one at home.

She regarded the two little girls with curiosity. The elder was beautiful, with fair hair, and even though she was rather unwashed she made a favourable impression. The little one was pale, badly dressed, and seemed to have rickets, or some childish wasting disease.

'Little girls,' said Frankojannou, 'what are you doing here? Where is your mother?'

The elder one answered,

' 'Ome.'

'At home,' interpreted the old woman. 'But where at home? Here or in the village?'

'Shiz not 'ere,' said the little one.

Apparently she was following the orders of her father, who wanted to prevent passers-by from disturbing the sick woman. In fact she was inside the hut, although the shutters were closed, perhaps so that the evening air from the river should do her no harm. It seems her husband had just gone

56

down into the neighbouring field a little while ago, to do a little extra work, and he had not bothered or not thought it worthwhile to shut the gate of the garden plot.

Old Hadoula asked another question:

'And is your mother in the village? What are you doing here on your own?'

'Daddizzeer,' said the little one.

'Where?'

'Down there,' she pointed.

'And what's he doing?'

The little child shrugged her shoulders. She did not know what to say. Finally, she offered:

'Eeezworkin.'

'What's your name, little girl?'

'Me? M'souda' (for Myrsouda).

'And your sister?'

'Toula' (for Asetoula).

Frankojannou thought it over. 'Will they shout? Will they be heard? How could they? Better do it quick,' she added to herself. 'He'll be back here in a while, wherever he is, it will get dark, he won't see to work down there. And I'd best be off as soon as may be without him seeing me any more than he saw me up to now.'

She hesitated a moment. She was conscious of a frightful interior struggle. Then she said, almost aloud. 'Take heart . . . it's decided.'

And grabbing the two little girls in her two hands she gave them a powerful push.

There was a big splash.

The two little creatures were floating in the water of the cistern.

The elder girl uttered a piercing cry that re-echoed in the evening loneliness.

'Ma . . .'

With an instinctive movement, Frankojannou turned her

face to the white cabin, to which her back had been turned until that moment.

She was ready to flee but she shot a glance at the cistern to see if the agony was long-lasting.

She took up her basket, which she had left on the ground, and took two steps away.

The two little creatures were choking in the water. The little one had already sunk, the elder was struggling.

A few seconds later the old woman heard from behind her the noise of an opened door and a weak voice.

She turned. The door of the cabin had opened. The sick woman, the mother of the two little girls, pale and wrapped up in a woollen sheet like a ghost, was standing at her open door.

'What is it?' said the suffering woman with a shiver.

At this Frankojannou, with great readiness of mind, as she was standing two steps away from the cistern, flung down the basket she has just picked up, and began to run and leap and cry out.

'The girls . . . The little girls . . . they've fallen in! . . . Look . . . Christians, are you crazy? How did you come to do it? To leave them alone like that by the cistern, and full of water? Lucky I was here! I was just passing! It was God sent me.'

And bending over and pulling off her skirt, together with her 'woollen' or petticoat, and flinging off her thick old worn out slippers, she flung herself heavily with a great splash into the water of the cistern.

The sick woman had uttered a harsh cry. She ran down the two or three stone steps from her door, hardly able to walk from weakness, but still moving forward. Before she came up to the cistern, Frankojannou had hold of the smaller girl, who seemed to her likely to be already drowned, and drew her slowly out, with her head and face underwater. She lifted up the little body and put it on the stone rim, then bent and took

58

hold of the other girl, the elder one. She grabbed her by one foot and the hem of her dress; while the body came upwards, the head remained downwards and underwater for as long a time as possible.

At last the mother arrived on the scene, and Frankojannou dragged the body decisively out. She put it down beside the other body.

The two little creatures were senseless.

Searching the water with her feet, Frankojannou discovered with some effort the mouth of the cistern on the southern side, blocked by a broad plank with a tall handle like a stick, and setting her foot on this she climbed laboriously up to the rim, all dripping.

'You see! I never thought of it!' argued Frankojannou pointing. 'I should have pulled on that handle and opened the drain, and the cistern would have emptied at once before the little girls drowned, poor things!'

It was true that she had not thought of it. But it was a hypocritical piece of sincerity.

Frankojannou shook the hems of her clothes, which were soaking, and casting a glance at the two senseless bodies, she began to speak fast and forcefully.

'They need hanging by the feet. And beating with a reed to dry them out. Lucky the water isn't salty. Where's your husband, Christian? Leaving them like that, tiny little girls on their own, playing with the water in the cistern! Lucky I came. It was God sent me. I came by from Anagyro, from the olives. Just as well the gate of the plot was open!

'Where's your husband? Where is he? As I came through the gate I heard Splash! I ran! What could I see? I wasn't in time. I didn't even know you were here. I thought you were in the village. I heard you were ill. Oh what a shock I had. They need hanging upside down and quickly. I don't believe they're quite drowned. Where's . . . that man of yours? Where is he?'

Taking a strong hold of the smaller body, which she was fairly sure was already dead, she carried it over to a tree to hang it upside down, just as she said.

'Where's there a bit of rope? Look, I can see a cane with string. Good, we can do with that.'

She nodded impatiently at the sick woman to bring her the reed that the two little girls had been playing with so little time ago.

The woman, dazed and beside herself, wringing her hands in despair, spoke in a weakened voice:

'But where's their father?'

'You're asking me?' said Frankojannou.

'Wont you shout? I can barely speak, my heart isn't working, my dear. He may be down there in the field.'

Frankojannou put down the little body for a moment on the ground; she ran a few paces to untie the cane with the string, to try to undo it or to cut it, to fasten the feet of the little drowned girl to the branch of the cherry tree, and hang her body upside down.

At the same time, in reply to the woman's appeal, she yelled out in a wild, strange voice:

'Ianni! Ianni!'

Her shout resounded along the valley. But no Iannis appeared. Frankojannou tried the little girl's feet and tried to hang her up, continuing to shout as she did so.

'Ianni! Where are you? Come here! The girls have fallen in the cistern!'

'Better he should take his time,' she said to herself.

'Can't he hear, this Christian man? So stuck to his work! It's after dark now. Ianni! Ianni!'

At the same moment she realized she had nearly given herself away, because the woman had not told her Iannis was at work in the field, she had seen him herself, and if anyone had told her it was the drowned child. So she put in:

'But where is he? Did you say in the field? What's he doing

there? My dear, who can run down there? You're a sick woman. Ianni, where are you Ianni?'

In the end they heard a voice from a distance, from beyond the furthest hedge.

'What is it? Who's shouting?'

'Run, Ianni. The girls have drowned!' the sick woman roared out painfully.

In a minute Iannis came running.

In the meanwhile Frankojannou had hung up the first little body and picked up the body of the elder child. She was feeling it with both hands, to make sure it was already dead. At the same time she threw a sidelong glance at the unhappy mother, pale and shivering under her white, woollen sheet. She shook her head in unwilling pity.

When she saw the father, the gardener, running towards them, she turned the body head downwards and held it like that for some time, doubtful and afraid.

'What is it? What's up?' shouted Iannis distraught.

'There! Lucky I was here,' shouted Frankojannou. 'I was on the way from Anagyro with my basket. I thought I'd give you some herbs I collected today in the ravine, to make a potion for your wife. I heard she was ill. Lucky the gate was open. I came in. I heard a splash. The shock it gave me! The two little girls were playing fishing-rods and they fell in the cistern. As far as I could see they were quarrelling about who was to hold the rod and catch fishes. The little one tried to snatch it from the big one. The big one gave her a shove and pushed her into the water, but the little one had grabbed hold of her and seems to have dragged her into the cistern as well.' (Frankojannou had made up this impromptu explanation out of the air and by inspiration.) 'Ach! The shock I had! I heard a splash! Lucky I was here! It was God sent me! Oh dear, Oh my Christians, little girls like that to be left alone to play by a cistern full of water!'

Iannis, seeing the two senseless bodies in the pale rays of

the dying sun, tore at his hair, and bit at the joints of his fingers, and answered.

'Oh! What a sin! You're right, my Christian woman! Ach! What a thing to happen! And I was down in the field pulling greens. And I couldn't rest, poor idiot! Something was eating me! And I never thought of the cistern being full! And I was frightened, I was worried there was something. I said to myself I'd leave the picking and come back, run back to the plot. And I said it's the Devil, he's digging me some hole, he's cooking up something against me. And I never had the sense to drop the work, poor idiot. Och! You're right, however you say it, my dear. Ach! Ach! What a sin.'

And in great distress, the gardener helped with the remedies against drowning that the experienced Frankojannou knew.

Old Hadoula had to stay all that night in the cabin, where she experienced the rare and indescribable sensations of a murderess transformed suddenly into doctor to her own victims. With all the hangings and rubbings that she ordered, the two little girls were dead. In the morning Iannis ran into town to make his declaration to the authorities, while Frankojannou stayed behind to keep the sick mother company in her tears and lamentations, and to do the work both of consoler and healer.

The justice of the peace and his colleague, the police magistrate, came out to the spot. Frankojannou, under questioning, told the tale of her expedition the day before, and her chancing to pass by the vegetable plot. She then repeated more or less word for word what she had said to the father of the two little girls. 'The little one tried to snatch the rod from the bigger one. The big one gave the little one a shove, and pushed her into the water, and the little one had grabbed hold of the big one and seems to have dragged her into the cistern as well.' She brought this out rather as guesswork, because she had only just set foot inside the gate, she said, when she heard a splash, and she wasn't in time to prevent the catastrophe, she just got 'a terrible shock'.

The resident doctor came and saw the corpses, and composed his report; it was apparent that the two girls had been drowned by falling into water.

No suspicion existed against Frankojannou. A priest came by and read a service over the two little creatures, at the chapel of Saint Anthony. They buried them out there among the reeds and bushes, close to the north wall of the chapel.

10

The Easter festival passed by. One day in Low Week old Hadoula was doing some washing with the help of her little daughter Krinio, in the big courtyard of Mr Alexander Rosmais. He was a distinguished old man, her relation by marriage and the godfather of nearly all her children. In the covered part of the yard called the Oilery, beside the huge wooden press like Noah's Ark in a picture, near the well, and where the enormous mulberry tree in new leaf extended its vast green branches like a cruciform blessing upon worthy and unworthy, the little garden with its wooden fence displayed its intoxicating multicoloured flowers for the sweet refreshment and delight of the eyes of all the creatures of God. Beside the little oven with the artificial cistern for the vintage, Frankojannou had her great, deep trough, and Krinio had another beside it, and there for two days the two of them had washed and bleached and rinsed and spread out and dried and gathered in tirelessly, and still they were not at the end of the work they had to finish.

On the second day Frankojannou had been much annoyed by the running and tricks of a noisy swarm of little boys and girls who invaded the courtyard to disturb her. Nearly all the children of the neighbourhood, ten or fifteen in number, pushed into the yard, ran about, jumped and danced, chased round and round the press, played hide and seek, and bent over the well. They were Narcissi eager for their own reflections and in the same danger of falling into the water. Little girls, uttering loud, inarticulate cries like so many

64

Echoes, ran to hide behind the oil-press, in dark corners, wherever playful fear enchanted them. All their pranks took place with a vast childish indifference to any question of leaving the industrious old woman and her daughter to do their work in peace.

The courtyard had two gates, a big one and a small one. Frankojannou had shut them both continually with the bar or the bolt, hoping for peace and quiet, but each time in a little while they were both open again. This was because the inhabitants frequently went in or out, and it was not only the children who came in from outside, but relatives and friends of the house as well. She complained to the reverend lady of the house, who continually scolded the children, quite in vain. She complained to the two neighbours, who were mothers of some of the noisy children. They replied she should look to her own work and not interfere with other people's lives.

When it was close to noon, Frankojannou sent Krinio home to get bread and beans for lunch, which she had told Amersa to boil, since Amersa always did her work in the house, and was not accustomed to take part in washing or other outdoor tasks.

Frankojannou was left alone for a time, and she went on washing. At that hour there were only two or three little girls in the courtyard. They made just as much noise as the boys. Since the foundation of a girls' school in the village these little girls had been very much awakened. The lady teacher did not teach them a lot of reading and writing, and still less of handicraft. She only taught them 'to take confidence' and not 'act terrified' or 'like mountain girls', and proclaimed that it was time for them to be 'emancipated'.

Frankojannou scolded them continually, but they did not listen. One little child hardly seven years old began to mock the old woman with mimic gestures of her hands and mouth.

For a moment, the two other girls ran out of the courtyard,

and Xenoula, who was left alone, bent over the well and tried to reach the water to stir it with a stick. She bent and bent, but the stick was very short and would not reach.

'Eh, my God, and if you fell in, Xenoula!' said Frankojannou with a strange laugh. 'What a relief it would be to your mother!'

'Eh, my Gott, an' if you fell in!' imitated Xenoula in a parody of her voice. 'What a relief to your mutter!'

She had raised herself up a little, and now she bent down deeper than before.

The square mouth of the well was fenced round with boards of an uneven width, so that the sides were not the same height. The little board where Xenoula was leaning was lower than the other three. It was rotten and slippery, and worn away by the rubbing of the bucket-rope for pulling up water. Its nails were rusty, it was unsound and moved. As the little girl bent down, she put the whole weight of her body on her left hand resting on the board. She slipped, the board gave, it came away at one end, and Xenoula fell headlong into the gaping mouth of the well. There was a drowned cry, and then a great splashing in the water.

The surface of the water was a fathom and a half below the mouth, and the depth of water must have been a fathom.

With an instinctive movement, Frankojannou wanted to shout out and run to help. But she drowned her own shout in her throat before it was uttered, her movements were paralysed and her body froze. A strange thought came into her mind. She had just uttered the prayer, more or less as a joke, that the child should fall into the well, and look it happened! So God (did she dare to think?) had heard her prayer, and there was no need to move her hands any more, enough for her to pray, and her prayer was answered.

After a moment, she decided to go to the well mouth and bend over and look into the depth. She saw the agony of the little girl, unable to breathe in the water, and said to herself that even had she wanted to, she could not have saved her. Yet certainly, if she drowned . . . they would blame her. It was late now to shout for help. Too late to save the child, but probably not too late for her to show her innocence. Still, she could not make up her mind to shout. It would have been better if she had shouted at once. But what bad luck! Her sin had taught her about luck. If Krinio were here now, what a bit of luck it would have been! She would certainly have been able to go down barefoot into the water, since the well, as usual, had steps on its inner walls, footholds built into the stones. They could be very dangerous and slippery, but Krinio might probably have succeeded in saving the little girl. But now it was despair and death!

Frankojannou had briefly forgotten her first idea, that God had willed for her prayer to be heard and the child to be drowned. Now the thought came back to her and unintentionally she laughed a bitter laugh.

In the twinkle of an eye she decided what she ought to do. I'll go home, she said to herself. I'll say, since Krinio was late coming — maybe the food wasn't ready — and I was very hungry and I preferred all of us to eat at home. To save Krinio the trouble, and to give myself a rest.

And in a moment, she put her trough with all the clothes she still had half-washed behind the olive press in a big wooden store-place. This she locked and put the key in her pocket. Then she went running out of the yard by the little gate, which she shut behind her with the latch. And off she went.

11

When Xenoula's body was drawn up from the well drowned and dead, old Hadoula was no longer at peace, cold fear began to crush her. This time, she thought, even though she was not at fault, she would not escape.

In fact the authorities had begun to be suspicious. The coincidence was too great. This old woman had played a minor part at the drowning of Iannis Perivolas' two young girls at Mammo's brook. Although they had seen no signs of guilt or even hints of suspicion then, the whole story was paradoxical and strange. Now the same old woman had been in the courtyard of old Rosmais at about the time when little Xenoula, the daughter of Propantis, was drowned in the well. This gave the justice of the peace some ground for suspicion. He drew this to the attention of his colleague, the police magistrate. As public prosecutor, his colleague limited himself to speeches at penal sessions, such as 'According to the witness of the witnesses it appears that he did, or appears that he did not do this act'. For the rest he took no opportunity to widen his effectiveness or exercise his tongue. So he simply replied that 'since the justice of the peace said so, so it was, and so it appeared to him'. And then the two of them decided to subject Hadoula the widow of Iannis Frankos to the most severe questioning, and if need be proceed to her personal arrest.

The first questioning had taken place on the spot and had been perfunctory. The justice and the magistrate had not yet conceived their suspicions, or else they had not yet communicated them to each other. (The agreement of the one, as always happens, increased the conviction of the other ten-fold.) Frankojannou had given her evidence about the events we already know and without any sign of their inner significance. She said that in the place where she was washing, 'as it was past mid-day and she was hungry, and her daughter Krinio had gone home to bring food, and as she was late, and she was very hungry too, and that crowd of boys and girls made her head go round, worrying the whole world with their games and their tricks in the courtyard, and round and round the oilery and round and round the oil-press and the well too, and at her own sensible warnings those badly brought up children had mocked her and joked at her and made her lose her patience – all of this her daughter Krinio confirmed – then she, with her head spinning and unable to stand on her feet from hunger, decided to go home, so they could all eat there together, and to save Krinio from the needless labour of bringing the food, and to have a little peace and rest for a moment. So she went out of the courtyard and shut the gate with the latch. After lunch, about an hour later, when they came back to the courtyard, she and Krinio, at first they had no suspicion of anything and went to work again. The children's noise had stopped for a time. But a little later when they needed to draw water from the well, Krinio's bucket had knocked on a solid body in the water, and she called to her mother in fear and amazement. Then the two of them together discovered the little girl's body floating or rather sunk in the water'.

Krinio was completely sincere in confirming this. The justice of the peace heard her deposition with a kindly ear. But at the same time he made a grimace at her mother. Frankojannou disliked that grimace – the 'ugly mug' of the justice – since she was a very experienced woman, and from that instant a deep anxiety possessed her.

In the house of her daughter Delcharo, where she was to be

69

found a little before sunset, she peered through the window anxiously again and again. She directed her glance to her own little house, which was visible although it lay to the side and not opposite. It stuck out beyond the few houses in between, since it was two or three feet further into the street. But mostly as she looked, Frankojannou saw nothing.

Her daughter Delcharo saw how worried she was and began to look out too. As the sun was setting she suddenly shouted to her in fear.

'Mother! Mother!'

'What is it?'

'Come and look!'

'What?'

'Two regulars standing outside the courtyard and staring up at your house.'

Old Hadoula rose and saw what she had feared. Two 'regulars', or village policemen, just as in the days of her son the Moron about fifteen years ago when he had dragged his mother by the hair along the cobbled road and knifed his sister. They were standing there waiting and watching the house closely.

Frankojannou realized that the evil which threatened her was great and immediate.

'I must go to the mountains, daughter!' she said suddenly. 'If I'm in time.'

'Why, mother?' asked Delcharo distressed.

'Because they're after me to put me in prison.'

'Really? Was it you, mother, who threw the girl in the well?'

'No, God's my witness! I didn't do it,' said Frankojannou.

'Well then?'

'Quiet!'

'The sin is tracking you down, mother,' said Delcharo afraid.

'Quiet! Have you gone mad?' said her mother grimly,

suspecting an insinuation in the tone her daughter used to her.

'What can I say, poor creature that I am!' said Delcharo, wringing her hands helplessly.

'Ah! Don't say that! No! You mustn't say it!'

And she went quaking down the stairs to run away.

'Where are you going, Mother?'

'To the mountains, I told you. Give me some rusks.'

Delcharo ran to open the cupboard and took out a few rusks.

'And give me my basket, and a knife,' went on Franko-jannou in a violent tone. 'And throw me in a woollen wrap, and my kerchief and my old slippers. And give me my stick. Look and find it!'

Silently, patiently, Delcharo tried to carry out all these preparations.

'Where will you go, mother?' she said in tears. 'Oh, my heart's breaking!'

'Don't cry! I'll hide somewhere, I'll find a hole somewhere. Be quiet now, be sensible. Until the wrath of God passes.'

She took her stick and her basket and went silently downstairs. She made the sign of the cross.

Suddenly she paused on the third step and turned and spoke to Delcharo:

'You know what to do? I'll go by the upper road and get away, so those dogs won't see me. And at the same time, you run to the house, pretend you don't see them, the regulars, and shout up to Amersa from down on the road: Amersa, is mother up there?

'No, don't say Is mother up there? Just say, Amersa, how's mother? Is she better? Has she got up? Is she still in bed? So that they think I'm up there in the house and not well. So they don't suspect anything and don't chase after me, the dogs. Run, quickly!'

Then she added:

'Good luck — meet again!'

Immediately after that Delcharo went out as well. She ran light-footed, headed for her mother's house, and carried out her orders.

Frankojannou took the upper road to Kotronia with galloping feet. At the last echo of 'meet again', she added to herself unwillingly and with bitter irony, 'Either I shall meet you here or I'll go and meet your brother in prison, or your father in the next world — and that's the most certain of all.'

As she panted up the rocky hill, she said inwardly, 'Come on, come on, holy virgin! Even if I am a sinner.' Then in her innermost soul she said, 'I didn't mean to do evil.'

Hardly had she gone a few steps, when she saw someone on the rocks where the road went downwards towards the shore, among the last scattered houses of the town. It was Kyriakos the police sergeant, his fez with the little plume, his twisted chestnut moustaches, his short club in his hand with the inscription running round it. 'Strength of the Law'. With him there was an old veteran in military uniform. They were approaching the beach by a little side road and in a short time they would certainly have overtaken her or come up behind her.

Maybe it was chance that brought Kyriakos and the veteran to that spot. But the guilty woman was worried at the sight of them and hastened her steps. It seemed to her that they did the same.

Then as Frankojannou got to the seashore, by good fortune she suddenly saw before her the open door of a house, the house of a close acquaintance, and she did not hesitate a second before crossing the threshold. In her fright, she shut the door behind her with latch and bolt.

'Marouso, are you up there?' she asked in a loud whisper, as she climbed the stairs.

A short little ruddy-coloured woman came out of a bed-room door and made her appearance smiling, but with a worried look.

'Where in the world, Aunt Hadoula?' she asked.

'Don't ask, my child. I've had a great trouble,' Franko-jannou began.

Then she asked anxiously,

'Anagnostis isn't here?'

'No, he's not here. He doesn't come so early. He's in the cafe . . . Ach! Aunt Hadoula, I was just thinking of coming up to the house, to tell you the news . . . '

'Did you hear any?'

'They were saying yesterday afternoon, my master and his godbrother, Ayimeriti, who came to smoke a pipe and chat as they always do . . . '

'And what did they say?'

'The justice and the police magistrate want to take you in. They said they'd be sending the constables. They suspect you about the little girl who was drowned yesterday in the well.'

'Oh, the shock!'

'And I said I'd come and tell you, so you could hide, if you can. But what are you doing here?'

Frankojannou told her she had understood after her questioning the day before that the justice 'had her in his gunsights'. She was frightened of trouble and it was unjust. She'd seen the police spying out her house from her daughter Delcharo's house, where she happened to be this evening; so she decided to run away to the mountains. Then as she was coming down here along the shore, thinking of taking the hidden path up the mountain at the back of Kotronia, she saw Kyriakos, the sergeant, with an old regular coming up behind her. By the grace of God she was just passing Marouso's house, and Marouso, Frankojannou had the wit to add, had known her troubles in the old days. So seeing the door open, she had rushed inside to find a refuge.

'I locked the door from inside, my child . . . I was in such a state, what could I do? It was in my stars to suffer, and suffer I have. Marouso dear, may you have blessings: could you just

73

peep very, very carefully through that window? And see whether Kyriakos is down there, or whether he's gone off?'

Marouso went to the window she indicated and looked down at the road. Then she turned and said,

'He's further on, over there. Standing in the road with an old veteran. They're talking to our neighbour, Frankoulis the fisherman.'

'And are they looking this way?'

'They're looking at the sand over there.'

The old woman was terrified and held her hand to her face, as if to tear out her hair or scratch open her cheeks.

Marouso pitied her.

'Why don't you sit down, Aunt Hadoula? Don't be afraid. Whatever it is, it passes. Sit down there and I'll make you a coffee.'

Frankojannou flung herself distractedly onto a low stool in the kitchen doorway where they were talking.

The house appeared to belong to a well-to-do family, it had a number of rooms and good furniture.

'Don't you remember what happened to me, Aunt Hadoula?' said Marousa mysteriously, and her face became even redder than it was already. 'Remember what shocks, what agonies I went through then! And bless you, how you helped me! And your troubles will pass just like mine.'

'That's why I said you know my troubles,' replied Frankojannou modestly.

'It's my troubles I was talking about,' corrected Marouso truthfully.

She boiled up the coffee and poured it out.

'My master will be coming. Drink your coffee. And dip a bit of bread,' she added, cutting a big slice of it.

The old woman began to dip the bread and to chew it without appetite.

'Bless you,' she said. 'It doesn't go down, my child. With the cholic I have. My palate's making poison.'

Then she added:

'Could you take the trouble and look through the window again, outside? Is Kyriakos still down there?'

Marousa obeyed.

'He's there, Aunt Hadoula. He's deep in conversation with Frankoulis.'

'So now where am I to go? Has your father come? The sun's set. It's dusk. It'll be night.'

Marousa looked for a moment, then she said:

'I owe you a great favour, Aunt Hadoula. How could I forget it!'

'You remember?' said the old woman, smiling in spite of herself.

'Could I ever not? I'll do what I can, I'll do it for you.'

'Bless you.'

'It seems to me the best thing is if I hide you here for the night, now before my master comes.'

'Where?'

'Down below in the little cellar, on the sofa . . . you know?'

'Ah,' said Frankojannou, as if some recollection had come back to her.

'And at midnight when the cock crows . . . '

'Eh?'

'Before daybreak, whenever you feel . . . '

'All right!'

'If you like, get up and good luck go with you, wherever God guides you.'

'Please God,' said the old woman with a sigh.

'And the next night again, if you don't find another refuge that's better hidden and safer, come and throw a pebble at that window or the little balcony on the sea side, and I'll come down and open up and hide you in the cellar again.'

'Right, but just have a look, has Kyriakos gone?'

Marousa went beyond the half-wall to the window that

overlooked the road; she stayed there a little while; perhaps it was dark now and she could hardly make out much; then she returned.

'They haven't gone. The three of them are there.'

'Now there's one thing I don't know,' said Frankojannou thoughtfully. 'I don't know if Kyriakos saw me come in here or not. If he hasn't seen me and isn't in ambush for me, I'd do better to make off, and take the pressure off you at once.'

She said this sincerely. She was distressed, she longed for the mountain air. Up there she felt she would find relief, and she hoped safety as well.

'However it is, you mustn't go this evening,' said Marousa, becoming more eager as memory warmed her. 'Stay tonight, Aunt Hadoula, in the little cellar, and let me remember my old sufferings. Will they come back and visit me like a dream when I sleep?'

'That's how one remembers them later, my child,' said the old woman with a cunning openness. 'Ach, every sin has its sweetness!'

'True, and what bitterness it brings in the end!' finished Marousa gloomily.

The house was double. Apart from the principal building, there was a little annexe to the north, where the kitchen was, and beneath the kitchen the 'little cellar'. It was down there, by way of the trap and the little steps, that Marousa led her guest, before Anagnostis, master of the house, should come home. She brought her bread, a bit of cold stew left over from dinner, cheese, water and a glass of wine, and established her on the sofa of the small cellar, which was used as a store room for various household possessions. She spread her an old blanket, a worn goatskin, and a little sheet, put out a tough pillow for her stuffed with stalks of flax, and wished her goodnight and 'sleep lightly'.

Whether light or heavy, it was not possible that Frankojannou's sleep should be easy or pleasant, when she was so disturbed and so frightened. But her surroundings made her almost forget the present for a while and her own terrible position, as she recollected the past. What Frankojannou had twice modestly referred to as 'her troubles', and Marousa had sincerely acknowledged as her own 'troubles' and 'tortures', had happened eight or ten years ago.

Mr Anagnostis Benidis, who was childless, had adopted Marousa, and brought her up as strictly as his wife, buried fifteen years, could ever have done.

Mr Benidis in his day was the most important person in the place. He had been a village elder before the War of Independence, a delegate at the first Assemblies of Troizen, Pronoia, Argos and so on, and major before the Constitution. Then after the Constitution he was a senior official in a number of places. He had taken on Marousa, who was a Jewess, or as others had it Turkish, when she was scarcely more than an infant, and baptized her. Then, when he came home to draw his pension for a few last years, he had married her off to a cousin of his, and given her for a dowry the little annexe house — in the lower level of which Frankojannou was now hidden — with sufficient agricultural land and some ready money, promising to leave her the main house as well, with everything in it, when he died.

The son-in-law, once he had a child, was always away. He travelled on ships as a quartermaster. He was a famous sailor, but spendthrift and thoughtless. Recently he had been three years away from home. Meanwhile old Anagnostis had been widowed, and his adopted daughter, in the absence of her husband, served her adopted father continually in the house. She had been used to doing that since childhood. Her husband wrote letters from time to time, promising to come, but he never came. Marousa's daughter was already four years old, and still the father had never seen his child, nor did the child know its father's face.

At that time, with the development of trade and of the

community, the manners of this small, provincial spot had also begun in some way to develop. Strangers coming from other parts of Greece, which were 'more civilized', government officials or merchants, brought with them new and liberated theories. They called shame and self-control corruption, and lust 'natural things'. The unhappy Marousa, who had not been born in the place, was not very severe or ultrarespectable to begin with, and she had a slight streak of lightheadedness.

At the time, there were to be found on the island a clerk to the justice of the peace, unmarried and kilted; a harbourmaster's clerk, in breeches, who was an officer in the Marine Commissariat and an old play-boy; a dandy officer with an income three times his salary; and two or three agents of foreign trading companies and resident visitors of various kinds. They all kept perpetual company with two or three other youthful commercial dandies with plenty of affected, complimentary phrases on the tip of their tongues. A number of women were compelled to be in constant touch with these last, because of the inevitable and endless shopping from which it is impossible that the world of women should ever be separated.

Marousa could not escape from so many snares set in her path, so many siege-engines set around her walls by these merchant adventurers, and soon afterwards, in the absence of her husband, she was pregnant. She knew it when she was only two months gone. But before she discovered it, the whole neighbourhood knew of course, and maybe even before it happened. Only Mr Anagnostis was left in ignorance. 'It was a noise in the world,' as malicious Kokkitsa, one of the neighbours said, 'and he lay quiet on his pillow.'

There were evil tongues that said, without the least likelihood of course, that Anagnostis was applying David's old method, and seeking 'a new youth' through young breath and hot blood. But the said Kokkitsa and two or three other lady neighbours, who talked quietly and laughed loudly between themselves, were assured that 'Many have part shares in that child'. Its head should be the kilted clerk's with the amazing fez and the long pompom; the middle must surely be the jolly policeman's, and one foot (the one in the grave) the old devil's in breeches, and one hand (a grasping one) the customs man's and the other (a pretty little hand) the retail merchant's with the la-di-da language.

The said Kokkitsa was the first person Marousa covertly invited to share her secret. However uncomplicated Marousa appeared, she had noticed long ago that Kokkitsa suspected something. A direct confidence, Marousa thought, would flatter her and she could then persuade her to silence — by bribery if necessary. Marousa fell on Kokkitsa's neck 'to make her a sister under God and to put herself in her hands'. She begged her to be merciful, asked if she knew of any remedies which might banish the fruit of sin and may God be gracious! Because otherwise she would surely jump into the sea and drown, as it was near enough. Just below the house. And what good was such a life to her anyway! Kokkitsa calmed her down with words of comfort. She applied various ointments and poultices, but these had no effect at all.

The second person to be asked in was Stamato, a poor widow, and her sister Kondylo, both Albanian speakers from one of the islands in the Saronic gulf. They practised massages on the body of the unfortunate woman. She paid all three with what she stole from Anagnostis' houshold money. They thus prolonged the ointments and protracted the massages, quite uselessly.

One evening they were talking it over together in Mrs Thomais' courtyard, a few houses away, where the widow Chiono and aunt Kyranno had also gathered, all of them refugees from Macedonia from 1821. The first three gave a regular report every evening to Mrs Thomais and the two other old ladies, and they were all roaring with laughter.

Stamato's broken Greek, as she described the state the pregnant woman was in ('She's all short, and she have her feet short! She not drop him, do she? . . .') made them laugh longer. Old Kyranno added her own notes to Stamato's accounts in Macedonian dialect.

'They're dirty animals, I say! Pigs, yes they are! Not in our villages! Let her make him one, and I tell you where she'll have it, she'll have it in the cattle-market.'

Last of all Frankojannou, who knew more than all the others, was summoned to help. Marousa had begun to despair of the first three 'nurses'. She took refuge in Frankojannou as a last hope. And indeed old Hadoula with the drugs and potions and the hot and cold drinks she gave her patient, and with massages which she administered with much higher skill than the others, succeeded in a few days in inducing an abortion. Mr Anagnostis never knew anything about it.

This was the old service and the gratitude the two of them had hinted at that day. These were Frankojannou's 'old troubles' and those were Marousa's 'tortures'.

The memory occupied Frankojannou's mind while she lay on the sofa in the dark. Her hostess had not brought her a lamp, she had only left her a candle-end and a few matches. Frankojannou went right through the old story, and sleep would not come. Searching her conscience, she found one thing: whatever she had done then or now, she had done it all for the best. She curled up under the woollen cover, on her right side, let her head fall on her breast and tried to lose herself, to numb herself, to make oblivion come to her. Then, after all those years, she remembered the short prayer that an old confessor had urged her to recite often, 'Lord Jesus Christ, son of God, have mercy on me.'

The frequent repetition of the prayer did its work. In a few minutes Hadoula's mind was benumbed and she fell asleep. But in her sleep — or was she awake, she hardly knew which — she seemed to hear within her, in her very depths, an infant's

80

voice crying and moaning in lamentation. It was like the voice of her little grand-daughter silenced a few months ago by her own hand.

The old woman woke with a shock, terror-stricken. She started up anguished yet rested. That short sleep had wiped away her nervous restlessness. She felt for and found the matches, lit the candle, took her stick and her basket, put her slippers into it, and barefoot, in her stockings, moved towards her escape.

12

Marousa had given her the key of the little cellar, she had said to leave by the private door and then to lock up from outside and take the key away with her. In that way she could use it again the next night if she came back. As for Marousa herself, if she needed to go down to the cellar, she would go the way she had taken her guest, by the inner steps and the upper door.

Frankojannou now felt utterly stunned. The confining cellar with its dank air had upset her. It was high time to breathe some mountain air, before the police could lock her up, maybe for life, in the wet and sunless dungeons of human justice.

As she went out, the lamenting voice of the infant, the tiny girl unjustly slain, moaned inside her. She stood in the doorway, peering carefully outside, right and left, up and down the road. Not a soul, not a shadow. She put wings to her feet. It was not the first time she had heard that sorrowful infant cry in the cavernous, echoing darkness of her soul. Now she thought she was escaping from danger and disaster, but she carried her wound with her. She imagined herself escaping from dungeons and prison, but prison and Hell were within her.

It was about two o'clock in the morning, a moonless, starlit night. The beginning of May, the second week after a late Easter. The countryside was fragrant, the breeze scented. A few sleepless birds sang matins in the branches. Frankojannou took the narrow, winding path she knew so very well, behind the gardens and below the rocks. The path was scarcely visible in the starlight. It was partly overgrown with projecting bushes of thorns and briars that sprouted from the garden fences. The agile old woman walked on green weeds and camomile and budding acanthus; she trod the uphill path like a girl, like a young mountain shepherdess.

On her right the long line of gardens and enclosed plots had ended, but on her left the small rocky hill of Kotronia still stretched away towards its three picturesque summits, one behind the other, crowned with windmills, little white huts and houses creeping round them. She was now at the place where the slope was still gentle. Vineyards began here and the fields with fruit-trees and olives. Then came the fields with high hedges shaken by the night breeze, where the rising slope began to be steeper. Frankojannou ran and ran, breathing lightly, her face whipped by the morning land-wind, the head-wind, beloved dawn-child of the North.

She hurried on as fast as she could to reach long familiar sites before the day broke. On the north coast of the island there were many bandits' lairs, untrodden spots, caves and rocks where wild herbs grew. There were colonies of kapparis and kritamon and brineherb, and day by day the flocks of kids and goats ruined the few paths that existed. Her refuge would be up there where her childhood memories were. Hadoula had been born on those northern shores, close to the wild blue sea, in the old Castle on its gigantic, sea-smitten rock. It was there she had been brought up until the age of ten.

Later when things quietened down and the new town was founded at the southern harbour, her mother the witch, so much hunted by the bandits and the Albanian gangs, had often taken her up there. She showed her all the lairs of the outlaws, the untrodden rocks and the caverns, and told her fantastical but true stories about every single place. It was in this region, when they married her off and set her up, and gave her 'the blessing of the dear departed', as her mother would have it, that they situated her dowry. The house, the deserted Castle, and the field at Bostani, on the untreadable crag. Later, when she was mistress of her own household and had learnt a good deal and made progress in the wisdom of women, she used to pick herbs and clover and snakeweed in the ravines and on the mountains. She had often visited those places in the course of her work.

So that was where she was heading now, if God should grant her a safe arrival. But in what terrible circumstances. And what would her luck be like from now on? Only God knew.

Before she reached the place where the road began to climb steeply, she came to an enclosure fenced in with dense briars and tall bushes and bits of circuit wall, inside which there were many kinds of fruit trees. Here Frankojannou happened to stumble on the road. She fell lightly, with a little noise, into a bush and she uttered a small sound like a groan.

From very close by, but from the other side of the hedge, she suddenly heard the loud barking of a dog. She picked herself up and went on her way with quicker steps.

'Who can it be?' she asked herself.

There came a rough and sleepy voice, but a commanding one.

'Eh! Out of the gardens! Outside! Outside!'

She recognized the voice of Tambouras the field guard. Then she knew what had happened. The enclosure by which she had stumbled belonged to the present Mayor of the place. Inside it, close to the other other trees, there were a few cherry-trees, with nearly-ripened fruit, sweet and black-looking in the starlight among dark green leaves. Tambouras had nothing else to guard, since it was not yet fruit time or harvest time, so he slept in the Mayor's garden in a little cabin with his dog, and guarded the cherries for fear the Mayor's electors should make off with them.

As she ran off she could still hear the dog barking; she

listened carefully, and she thought she could make out human footsteps. But she was mistaken. Perhaps it was the echo of her own feet. Apparently the field guard had only half woken, and uttered his usual shout mechanically, as if he was sleep-walking. Then he had gone straight back to sleep.

Hadoula disappeared up the slope in among the trees. There she stood still for a moment and listened again. She heard nothing but the calling of a bird, the buzzing of a night-time insect, the blowing of the wind. Then the cherries came into her mind. She had seen them dimly glistening on a loaded branch that hung outside the Mayor's garden. It had been near where she stumbled.

'Ach!' she said, 'and I didn't go and get a cherry to wet my mouth, which tastes filthy. I forgot to drink a drop of water before I left. I must get to a spring, I must.'

It was only now she remembered that she had not drunk any water before she left the cellar, where she had passed so few, yet such long, hours of agonizing. Hadoula brooded bitterly how everything in this world, down to the smallest of things, came to her at the wrong time and upside down. If she had thought in time to steal a few cherries from the Mayor's cherry tree, she would have trodden carefully, approached cautiously. Then perhaps the field guard would never have woken. Nor the dog barked. But she had had to be careless and inattentive, not to watch where she was walking, she had to take a wrong step and make a little noise, enough to wake the dog and the man. Everything started like that.

Anyway, now her thirst had become intense after the uphill climb. She cut some olive leaves and put them in her mouth.

She walked another hour. Now dawn was breaking. After she got to the top of the hill, she went down again into the river-bed in the shadow of the mountain with the wrinkled sides called the Watches. Who knew what outlaws of by-gone years had kept their sleepless watch up there, and given the place its name? She got to the little spring at the foot of the mountain. It was already light. She drank water, freshened herself, and again she was off. People often came to that spot, shepherds and day-labouring peasants and so on. Frankojannou wanted to be seen as little as possible. She climbed further down, until she came to the deep stream at the bottom, which runs down to the sea. It is called Lechouni.

She got there a little before sunrise. There were two or three watermills there, rather old and useless, only one of them working, and that rarely. Everything indicated desertion, there was no trace of a human being to be seen. But Frankojannou was overcareful, she was unwilling to go near. She fled away from the place, walked on in cover, and got to a deep pool of clear water that few people knew. It was a secret, untrodden place. It formed a kind of cavern of grass and tree-trunks and ivy. The cave of a Nymph, of a Dryad of ancient times, or a Naiad who perhaps found refuge there.

Anyone who was going to get down into the small hollow in the ground where that pool of water was, would need fortune for a guide and the feet of Frankojannou, feet without shoes. Now they were split and bloody from the brambles and thorns. She sat and rested. She took the bread and cheese and a little meat that Marousa had given her out of the basket; in the evening she had been unable to eat anything, after the coffee she had drunk in the kitchen. All she had kept were the biscuits she had taken from her daughter Delcharo's house. She ate, she drank the refreshing water, and revived a little.

At that moment the sun rose. The great disc appeared to climb out of the waves of the distant sea just opposite. Hadoula could see a strip of it from her hiding-place. The birds of the rocky and echoing mountain which rose up behind her uttered their long cries, and the little birds of the valley, the scrub, the little wood, let loose their glittering melodies.

A warm sunbeam made its way from the distant flaming sea, into the dense foliage and ivy that covered the miserable old woman's sanctuary. It lit up the morning dew covering the rich emerald robe of earth until it glittered like an abundance of pearls. The sun chased away the coldness of the moisture and the chill of dark fear. It brought a moment of hope and of warmth.

Frankojannou took out the much folded woollen blanket from her basket, unfolded it, wrapped it round her, and laid her head on the root of an ancient plane tree. She fell asleep.

In her sleep she thought she was still young; her father and mother married her off in her dream as they had done in fact, and gave her 'the blessing of the dear departed' and the dowry, including her father's plot, where she had dug and watered cabbages and beans when she was little. And her father rewarded her for the hard work, and gave her 'four heads' out of the cabbages. Hadoula took the four plants happily into her hands, but when she looked, Oh horror! she saw they were four little dead human heads.

She stirred and awoke. 'Lord Jesus Christ!' she said. Again she fell asleep. She dreamt that her mother caught her red-handed searching for the treasure down in the cellar among the barrels and the great storage pots and the pile of firewood. When she saw her she smiled her bitter smile and to save her the trouble took out the treasure herself and opened it. Out of so many silver pieces jumbled together she gave her three German dollars, the kind that had the ikon of the Blessed Virgin on them, with the inscription Patrona Bavariae. Frankojannou took the three coins from her mother's hand with a mixture of joy and shame. But when she looked at them she saw that the three coins with the faces on them bore three little, darkened faces with eyes put out . . . Oh the shock! little girls' faces!

She woke shaking, unhappy, frenzied. It was already noon. The sun was burning above her head, up above the crest of the cool plane tree. With all the warmth of the sun and the glitter of the May light, the impression of the dream remained in her mind a long time. She thought it extraordinary that she had dreamed those dreams in daytime. In all the daytime sleeps she had ever had in her whole life, she never remembered having dreamt.

She wet two rusks in the stream, placed them on the flat stone by the lip of the pool, and forgot them there for a long time until they were loosened by the soaking and moistened through. After a time she filled the palm of her hand with the pieces and ate them.

When the sun hid behind the crest of the rock mountain and the valley lay in shadow and it was evening, she grew restless. She poked her head out of her hiding-place. She peered up and down into the valley overgrown with olive trees, but not a soul was to be seen. She took her basket and stick and left her tiny hollow. She climbed up to the copse and followed quietly along the course of the ravine. There she began to search for herbs, her old art, not knowing any more what use they would be since there was no other sanctuary left in the world for her but prison and solitude.

Yet she nourished an undefined hope that she might find hospitality at some sheepfold or shepherd's cabin, and then she would offer the herbs to her host's wife as a small exchange. But mostly she was gathering herbs to forget the grief which tormented her.

At that moment she heard the sound of a distant jingling, and in the distance she saw a flock coming towards her. If she was not quick to get out of the little gorge, her hiding-place would inevitably soon be discovered. Even if most of the sheep and goats scattered and went to drink at the big stream, which flowed down to the mill-pool and then on below the windmill, a few of them would certainly come to the little stream by the pool. Then the beasts would be startled and shy and go leaping away and the shepherd, whoever he was, would discover her and be amazed and possibly suspect something.

The best thing to do would be to confront the shepherd at once with the inevitable hypocrisy, the lie on her lips. Anyway it was quite likely a dweller in the wilds would have had no news from the town for days. He would have no knowledge of any pursuit of Frankojannou.

13

In a little while, Frankojannou came out of hiding and followed the stream, bending down this way and that in search of herbs. Then a flock of sheep with a few goats among them did indeed draw near, and the shepherd appeared. Frankojannou knew him at once. He was called Iannis Lyringos.

As soon as he saw the old woman in the distance he began to shout:

'And from where in the world, Aunt Garouphalias!' (Lyringos recognized the face but he seemed not to have remembered the name rightly.) 'Lucky I found you! It was God sent you!'

'What can be up?' said Frankojannou to herself. 'He has something to tell me. Surely the man won't have heard anything about what my troubles are.'

'Do you know something, Aunt Garouphalias?' continued Lyringos as he came nearer.

'What would I know, my son?' said Frankojannou hypocritically, taking care not to disturb the man's illusion about her real name. 'I've been out of the village since yesterday. I came to gather herbs in the ravines.'

'Listen, Aunt Garouphalias,' the man went on simply. 'We had a baby last night at the cabin.'

'A baby?'

'We've wrapped it up! It's the third little girl we've had in five years — all little girls, that's her luck.'

'May she live!' said the old woman. 'And a good recovery to

your wife.'

'So far as that goes, the little girl came sick into the world, she's always crying and she won't stick to the breast. And her poor mother isn't so well either. All fever and wasting, that's her luck!'

'Really?'

'If you'd do us the kindness and come by the cabin, and do some medicine, Aunt Garouphalias? That mother-in-law of mine isn't any use for anything; what good can she do?'

'But now it's nearly nightfall,' said Frankojannou cunningly.

And inside herself she said, 'It's my fate now! Och! My God!'

'Let night fall . . . If you want, you can sleep in the cabin.'

Frankojannou stood still as if she were hesitating. But she was fully ready to agree.

Just then as the last ray of the sun gilded the crest of the eastern hill with its many olive trees, and made their foliage gleam, two men appeared running down a path between the olive groves.

Frankojannou saw them first and trembled. The sun that lit up the leaves made the long unpolished buttons on their uniforms glisten. They were policemen.

At once Frankojannou turned her back on Iannis Lyringos and ran westwards towards the foot of the stony mountain.

The shepherd cried out in amazement,

'Where are you going, Aunt Garouphalias?'

'Quiet! my child,' she whispered in panic, 'for the love of Christ. It's regulars coming. Don't say you saw me!'

'Regulars?'

'Don't give me away, my child, or I'm lost! Be quiet! If I get away now, I'll come in the night to your cabin.'

She took off her slippers, which she had worn coming up from the pool, and dropped them into her basket. Light-footed and shoeless, basket on her left arm and stick in her

91

right hand, she flung herself straight up a steep crag. Only the goats among Lyringos' sheep would have been able to clamber after her.

In a few seconds she had climbed up ten or twenty feet. The first protruding rock hid her, and she was seen no more.

A few seconds later the two policemen reached Lyringos. To get to him they had been forced to descend and cross the stream through the same dense cover which Frankojannou had used to get away.

The shepherd was watching his sheep and goats, and shouting 'Tivi! Tivi! . . . oi! oi!' He was trying to collect them and take them uphill, to lead them to the southern ridge where his steading was.

The two men greeted Lyringos. Then they asked if he had seen 'that miscreated woman, what do they call her, Frankojannou'.

Lyringos said no.

One of the policemen insulted the shepherd.

'You're lying. I saw her.'

He insisted he had seen the shadow, the 'looks' or the 'motions', as he said, of the old woman, jumping like a cat up to the top of the crag. The other had not seen her and was not at all so sure.

The first one in his leather shoes tried to leap up onto the rock. But after three steps he came crashing down and hurt his knee a little.

Frankojannou had climbed the mountain of Kouroupi, northerly, rocky, untrodden, whose feet the sea-wave kissed and lashed. From the peak, a view opened out to the coast of Macedonia, Chalkidiki and great Athos.

The place the fleeing woman had now reached was called the Shell. Seldom did human foot tread here. Only when some nanny-goat wandered or got stranded here might a shepherd risk his life to climb up to that unapproachable look-out.

Frankojannou found a little cave all open to the view of the sea, and in that shelter she sat at ease. This was the Shell. It was nearly certain that no pursuer would catch her there. If by chance there was one daredevil enough to resolve on the rock-climb and achieve it, she had her line of retreat ready. She knew another path, inside the double crest of the stony mountain, that split the massive rocks apart. It was known only to the local goatherds; it led straight to their folds and their dwelling-places.

She sat in the hollow of the rock, with the roar and melody of the waves below her, and the clang of eagles and screaming of hawks above her head. As night spread out, the immense sky vault lit up with stars, and the fragrant air would have been enough to embalm even her troubles. The shell-shaped cave was only about three times a man's height above the waves, but the rock-face was so steep it was impossible for a mere mortal to go up or down. It was a place good only for leaping into the sea and drowning, if one had made that decision.

The old woman produced from her basket olives, cheese, and the few rusks she had left. She ate her supper. Fortunately her flask was full of water. She had filled it that evening at the pool.

She shut her eyes and began to hum to herself, murmuring a song like a lament, but she could not sleep. Her fears and phantasms returned and besieged her. Frequently she heard the moaning of the infant within her, deep in her bowels. In vain she tried to silence that mysterious crying with the rambling, complaining song that she murmured.

Mother I want to go, to go and fly away
and see my fatal door, my fate from far away;
in fate's dark kingdom, I will be walking there,
and I will find my fate and I will ask of her . . .

It came into her head that maybe the regulars would hunt

her even at night. Suppose they climbed up to the sheepfolds and spent the night there? Had the shepherds not got green cheese? Had they not got milk and ball-cakes, or even chickens for slaughter and roasting on an improvized spit? And suppose that one of those shepherds was tricked into showing the police the inner path, would her retreat not be cut off? And it was infinitely more difficult to go down the way she had come up, unless she grew wings on her feet and flew away . . .

She would have much liked to know what the two regulars had said to Lyringos, and what he had answered. She knew his cabin, it was up on the ridge, behind the mountain, more than twenty minutes' away. But now of course Lyringos would have heard why she was being hunted down to be arrested, what she was accused of having done. So with what kind of face could she appear at the cabin? But probably he would not sleep at the cabin himself, more likely in his sheepfold which was somewhere not very far off. So then she would encounter the two women, the mother and the mother's mother, she would surprise them. What should she do? What should she decide?

She was numbed, and without completely sleeping she was dreaming. She thought she was elsewhere, somewhere different. Close to Saint John in Hiding, that Saint who healed hidden suffering and received the confession of hidden sins; suddenly she was there. She came to the garden of Perivolas, with his sick wife shut in the cabin. She saw the gate of the enclosed plot, the well, the cistern, the pulley. She clearly heard a cry coming out of the cistern, deep, very deep and strange. The water in the cistern was troubled, it was splashing like in a storm, it roared and almost spoke like a human being. She could clearly make out the word that the water muttered: 'Murderess. Murderess.'

She shivered and woke, and found in her mind a single strange question like the questions of delirium. 'Does drowned blood cry out like blood poured out?'

Then at once she came to herself, and tried once more to pronounce the soothing words of the prayer. 'Lord Jesus . . .' At the same moment she recalled the forgotten words of an anthem, which she had heard sung many times in her youth by an old priest, 'Jesus sweetest Christ . . . Long-suffering Jesus!'

And sleep came to her again, deep and continuous. She dreamt then as if she were reliving all her past life. What was extraordinary was that she dreamt the continuation of her own dreams of the past day. She no longer dreamt her marriage or her dowry but her childbed, and she seemed to have her three girls all at once, Delcharo, Amersa and Krinio, all small, all the same age, like triplets. The three of them were helped up to stand before her and they wanted petting and cuddling and kissing. But suddenly their faces were transformed, they were no longer her three daughters. They took on all the characteristics of the three girls who were drowned, and suddenly they were hanging like a necklace round her neck.

I am Matoula, said one. — I'm Myrouda, the lickle one, lisped the other. — And I am Xenoula, said the third. — Kiss us! — Cuddle us! — We're your little girls. — You're our mother, you made us. — She's our mother . . . into the next world, added Xenoula sarcastically. — Dance us. — Give us mmm! — Sing us bye-byes! — Sing to us! — Nurse us!

The whole thing seemed so natural. Those three little girls were her children. A living, human necklace! Dead, and heavy from the water, and foaming. How would old Hadoula hold out for the rest of time, wearing that frightful necklace round her neck.

She woke up shaking and in a frenzy. She rose, took her stick and her basket, and resolved to get away from that place. Here in the hollow shelter of the rock, in the roar of the deserted shore, there were too many ghosts. The place was

95

haunted. 'I must get away from here!'

But more practical thoughts came back into her mind. If by chance the two policemen had discovered the hidden path, it would be best to run now before danger appeared. If she met them on the way, she could probably find a way out behind the masses of rock. Far worse if they shut her in here in this narrow place, at the Shell.

She ran along the uphill road among rocks into the star-light, and after half an hour she came panting to Lyringos' little house. She stopped to catch her breath, then she knocked at the door.

One thing alone was certain, that the two regulars wherever they might be were not in this cabin, where there was a woman who had just given birth and her mother keeping her company. If they had stayed the night on the mountains they would be in one of the sheepfolds.

The old woman, who was Lyringos' mother-in-law, was unable to sleep, just like Frankojannou some days ago in the same situation. She got up and asked:

'Who is it?'

'Iannis sent me,' answered Hadoula from outside the shut door, without telling her name, 'to do some medicine for the mother.'

'At this hour?'

'I couldn't come any earlier.'

'Where did you see him?'

'Down at Lechouni, in the ravine.'

The old woman drew back the bolt and opened the door.

'They don't know anything,' thought Frankojannou to herself. 'I still pass muster with them.'

As soon as she set foot indoors, she began to behave like the lady of the house. By the light of a lamp burning before an old ikon — a triptych with Christ in the middle and various Saints in the two wings — she went straight to the hearth. The mother's bedding was close by on the floor. Hadoula tried the fire and saw that it was half extinguished. She brought kindling and logs from a pile in the corner, and threw a few onto the fireplace, then she blew the ashes and relit the flame. She took a stewpot which was by the hearth, filled it with water, searched in her basket, drew out two or three branches of herbs, flung them in, and put the vessel on the fire.

Then, nodding towards the mother, she said quietly to the old woman:

'Don't wake her . . . When she wakes, then let her drink this.'

The old woman replied with a nod. Frankojannou went on blowing at the fire. The old woman was helpless; she wanted to ask Frankojannou yet again how she came to be there at that hour, but she did not dare. It had been a difficult birth, and she was frightened her daughter might wake up suddenly and be disturbed.

The baby, a little rag of life two days old come into this world of sins and tortures, slept in her cot, but her breathing was rough and noisy in the surrounding silence. From time to time, when the breathing became somehow more intense and the infant seemed ready to wake and scream, its grandmother sang it to sleep with one repeated syllable "Ki, ki, ki, ki!' and this monosyllable which appeared to be the beginning of the word for sleep, or else from the root of 'lie still', this mono-syllable, many times repeated, really did appear to have an extraordinary magic and authority.

Time went by. The birds had already spoken twice. The Pleiades had gone far beyond midheaven. From the crest of the ridge opposite, where there were other cabins inhabited by shepherds' families, distant calls could be heard. The cry of the birds in the hen-house of Lyringos' cabin replied to them at once.

The mother woke. Her own mother gave her a drink of the medicine Frankojannou had prepared.

'Cheer up, my girl,' said Frankojannou in a gentle voice.

97

'How did you come here?' said the mother.

She looked at her puzzled and had difficulty in recognizing her.

'It was God sent me,' said Fankojannou with conviction.

'Welcome,' said the old woman then. 'It was well you came,'

And really, though she had felt it strange at first, she had thought it over since and recognized that the presence of Frankojannou was a comfort in her loneliness.

14

With the first streak of dawn, the child woke and began to cry. Frankojannou took command again. She advised the mother to put the child to the breast, to try if it would take milk. At the same time there was a noise outside, and immediately afterwards a voice.

'Old woman! Old woman! Are you asleep?'

It was Lyringos calling his mother-in-law.

The old woman knew his voice, got up and ran to the door.

'Come and give me a hand,' said Lyringos. 'The boy's missing and I'm alone.'

Iannis did not seem to have thought of asking about how his wife or child were. He only felt a pressing need to shout to his mother-in-law to help him with his morning work with the animals, the turning out of the livestock, the milking and so on.

'One can't do it alone, bad luck! Need four hands!' he added in self-justification.

The old woman came running out. Frankojannou was left alone with the mother and baby.

The young woman was half-asleep again and had not really grasped that her mother was gone. In a few seconds she woke and said,

'Where's mother gone?'

Frankojannou, thinking it was better for the young woman to sleep and rest, and knowing that any reply offered to those in fever and babbling as if they were sleepwalking does more harm than good, gave no answer at all. The young mother went to sleep again at once.

Then the baby daughter began to cry very softly, moaning unbearably. Frankojannou forgot all the remorse she had felt so deeply under the black wings of her dreams. Once again she was torn by the claws of reality, and began to think inside herself:

'Ach, he's right, poor Lyringos . . . "all little girls, her bad luck, all little girls!" And what a consolation it would be for him now, and for his unhappy wife, if the Almighty took her straight away! While she's small, and leaves no great sorrow behind her!'

At that instant a minor stumbling point occurred to her; where were Lyringos' other daughters, the elder ones? Then she remembered that before coming up to the cabin where she was now, she had passed the door of another, smaller hut, built onto this one at ground-level. It was the old woman's little hut, Lyringos' mother-in-law's. It was there she felt she had heard sleepy breathing and snoring. That was where Lyringos' other daughters would be, with their young un-married aunt.

As if she were mad, caught in the delusion of a dream, she put out her hand towards the cradle in which the little one was howling. She made a gesture with her fingers — a motion of gripping and strangling.

Just as she was feeling a savage joy in strangling the little girl . . . it came into her mind she was unbaptized, and if she choked her, that was a double sin . . . For a moment the thought held her back, but yet she resolved to overcome this obstacle . . . Her hand was within a finger's length of touching the little creature's throat.

At that instant there came a voice, a step, a noise, on the little balcony outside, and the door, which Lyringos' mother-in-law as she left had not bolted but only pulled to, opened wider and wider, yielding to pressure from outside.

'Is this,' asked the man who now appeared, 'the house of

Lyringos the herdsman?'

It was a policeman, with his half-buttoned shirt open at the throat, his hat crooked, his moustache unkempt, and his cape doubled up long over his left shoulder.

Inside the cabin the lamp guttered before the ikons. The fire had sunk back again into ashes. The light that hung from the shelf above the grate had gone out. It was dark. Outside the sky had lightened, and in two minutes the sun would rise.

The man saw nothing inside but dim shadows. The mother in her bedding like a vague heap, the child moving and breathing in the vessel used as a cradle . . . and Frankojannou sitting there like a ghost and stretching her hand out towards the cradle.

Frankojannou remained with her hand held out. She was possessed with horror, fear, dizziness. In half a minute she came to herself and saw the terrible danger.

Just behind her was a small window looking north, rotted, rain-soaked and badly made. As if an explosion had blown her, she turned mechanically, drew open the window, and jumped out. She fell in grass and straw, and the thud of her fall was unheard. The low window was only three feet from the ground.

But she had forgotten to take her stick and her basket with her; they had been beside her on the floor. It was puzzling how badly she had lost her head. She remembered them only at the moment she began running. It occurred to her that, if possible, she might go back. Her pursuers might be blinded and never notice them.

All the same she ran and ran . . . she had reached the wood, and she knew all its many paths. She did not turn to look behind her. She was sure the two regulars would be slow to realized what had happened, slow to set off behind her.

In fact those two servants of the communal will did not immediately realize what had happened. The justice of the

101

peace had sent them 'urgently' after her. In this he had acted with his magisterial colleague, who always said yes to him, and also with the police commissioner, who never replied no to him. He had sent them to the distant house of Iannis Lyringos, to invite him to appear before the authorities. If necessary they were to bring him in by force, since from what had been reported on the previous evening in the town by two policemen, the said luminaries had conceived the suspicion that Lyringos was implicated in the affair of the escape of the woman Hadoula, widow of Iannis Frankos, Christian, carrier out of household tasks. The two military men said they had seen her fling herself up the crag of that stony mountain.

So that in the dark before dawn, after having slept for two or three hours, fully dressed in the basement of the town hall, which was full of beetles, centipedes and lizards, and was used as a police station (it was the terror of all the streetboys, the young crooks and the debtors of the town), the two policemen arose at the first whistle of their officer, picked up their capes, and set out for the mountain.

They were sent specially to bring Lyringos — and any other shepherd whom they might interrogate and who replied in 'muddled words', the justice had the forethought to add. But above all they were to sniff out the traces of Frankojannou, and to discover her person. To this end they had full authority to search all the folds and all steadings and examine every shepherd on the mountain. So that for better or worse they took their capes with them.

The first policeman pushed open the door of the little house and saw darkness and shadow inside. He heard the noise of the northern window opening, he saw rays of light entering from it, and then suddenly a dark body, short, dumpy and formless, shutting out those rays. Then he heard the faint thump of a fall. In the double light of the crossed rays from door and window he saw clearly the nursing mother lying on her couch.

102

'What's up here?' the man shouted in surprise.
The mother woke and spoke in a weakened voice.
'Mother, is it you? . . . Have you come?'

15

When Frankojannou, her sides heaving and her tongue hanging out, got up to the high plateau of Kampia, she stood for a moment and turned back to the hill she had ascended. She searched for any sight or sound, shadow or footsteps of a hunting dog, of a policeman. There was nothing to be seen. And yet she did not feel safe.

She stood there lost in concentration, and she reflected. She made a kind of mathematical calculation. She reckoned the least time that would be needed for the two regulars to recover from their amazement (she had not seen the second one, but she divined him), then to realize what had happened, and perhaps to ask questions. The young mother would have been frightened out of her wits. She would not have any idea what to tell them. After that would they perhaps run to the steading where Lyringos and his mother-in-law were? That would make them all the later. Then they would fling down their capes and set about pursuing her on foot.

But had they seen or could they guess just what path she had taken? Was it one they knew? And she hadn't run on one and the same track all the way. At first she had made to the right, as if she meant to go downhill, but then she had veered left and climbed — with all the disadvantage of an uphill road to put a person out of breath when she is pursued and has to run for it. But if she was heaving, were they not subject to the same weakness, young men though they were? Hadoula happened to know that one of those two young men suffered from asthma. Not long ago he had been begging her son-in-law to get the old woman to make him up some medicine.

Still, in spite of the service rendered, Frankojannou knew she ought not to expect any mercy from the policeman. The man was doing his duty. The attentions they might once have paid her, and the titles they might have called her by would be nothing, if ever she fell into their hands now. She had noticed before, in the course of those hazards and tortures she had been through on account of her son, that this kind of man gets angriest of all when the pursued resists, when he shows initiative. Much more so when she runs away, and they are forced to chase her until their souls are coming out of the wrong end. Oh, certainly they are right to be harsh then, and to turn into wild beasts. So Frankojannou, as she fled and compelled them to run after her, did not expect any mercy from them.

As she stood thinking, she heard steps behind her from the opposite direction. She turned and saw a man, a shepherd. Frankojannou recognized him. He was called Kambanach-makis. He was coming with his sideways walk and his dog behind him. It growled when it saw the woman. Its master shouted at it.

He saw Frankojannou and stood still. He was on the way from his cabin to his sheepfold. He stood before Franko-jannou, tall and dark, spare and broadbreasted, with hair and beard the colour of burnt straw, with a crook in his hand as tall as he was. He seemed to be grief-stricken and in great distress.

'Ah, where did such good come from!' he said in his rough and difficult pronunciation, grinding his teeth as he spoke. 'Soon as I a-thought of you, I a-found you, Mrs Jannou. It's Himself sent you.'

'What are you saying, my son?' said Hadoula in her hypocritical manner.

'Good I crossed you! I said, that's that good woman down

105

there from the village, the one knows medsins and chases off every filthy pestilence. But you don't know nothing, Mrs Jannou!'

'What's going on, my son?'

'A great curse on you, with your sympathy, Mrs Jannou. A tough, unfortunate misery! My wife, may it away from your worship, she went out at night to do her water, out of the cabin, Mrs Jannou, and back she comes bad and awkward. She went out a charm and comes back in a muddle, struck down, tongue out, unknowable. She was struck down, may it away from your worship. Her tongue hanging out of her mouth, lost her speech, and taken with an evil boiling and a freezing and a clenching. Lying half dying on her bed.'

'Really? Oh what a sin. And when did it happen?'

'Evening afore last in the night, at the mid of night, Aunt Jannou! May it away from your worship and by your sympathy. A charm she went out of the cabin, and she came aback struck down, wounded. Labour up to the cabin, now that I've crossed you, Mrs Jannou. Just to look and see what a state she's in. Devil, but you'll do her good. With your medsins you'll chase out every bad thing one by one.'

'And how did it come on her?' said Frankojannou.

'Who knows what sins, Mrs Jannou. Himself knows.'

Hadoula thought for a moment. Then she said,

'Good. I'll go by there just now.'

'A long life and good on your soul, Aunt Jannou!' said Kambanachmakis. 'It's Himself sent you.'

When Kambanachmakis had made off, Frankojannou thought how after all she now had a refuge, at least for the next night, and how it might be best if she hid for the day in some thicket or some cave, somewhere the police could never find her.

She took the downward path and descended into Agalliano's brook. She stopped to drink water at a spring. There she met an old monk, Father Josaphat, the gardener of the

106

Monastery of the Annunciation, which traced its venerable silhouette on the crest above the ravine.

Frankojannou had sat down to refresh herself beside the cool waterspring, resting her head on her hand. She appeared deep in thought, but she was in fact all attention, straining her ears and thinking every second that she heard the footsteps of the police.

Father Josaphat had come to fill a pot of water. Seeing Frankojannou he greeted her.

'What are you doing here, old lady? I see you thinking something over . . .'

'Ach! My son!' said Frankojannou. 'I have tortures and troubles.'

'There's no lack of tortures in this world, old lady. Whatever a man does, he can't escape them.'

'Ach! Father Josaphat,' said Frankojannou in a sorrowful outburst. 'If only I were a bird to fly away!'

'Who shall give me wings as a dove?' said Josaphat, recalling the psalm.

'I should like to flee away from the world, old man. I can't stand any more!'

'Thou hast fled far off and made thine abode in the wilderness,' the old monk said in his turn.

'A terrible storm has come down on me, old man, and I have a great depression in me.'

'May God preserve you, my daughter, from all despair and every tempest,' said Josaphat, continuing his psalm.

'From malice and evil gossip and envy no one can escape.'

'Drown O Lord and divide their tongues, because in the city I have seen lawlessness and dispute,' went on Father Josaphat.

Then, since his pot was full, he added, 'If you pass by the gardens, old lady, give me a shout and I'll let you have a lettuce and some beans.'

And so he made off.

In the evening, Frankojannou was at the Far Ridge, at Kambanachmakis' cabin. The shepherd's wife, a woman over thirty and mother of five children, was lying on the bed. She was in a miserable state. Her face was contorted with muscular spasm, her tongue was hanging out of her mouth, and she was uttering inarticulate cries.

'How did this come on you?' Frankojannou asked by gesture rather than by speech. The sick woman answered with a growl that had nothing human about it.

Frankojannou sat down by the hearth and busied herself boiling herbs for the sick woman. She no longer had her basket, but she had filled the folds of her dress with various tiny weeds which she had picked that day down by the valley streams.

The invalid's two little girls sat close by Frankojannou's knees wanting to be cuddled. Frankojannou stroked their chins and their throats so hard that it hurt them, and one cried out,

'Mother!'

But it was as if their mother did not exist for them, and the unfortunate creatures were not of an age to understand her absence let alone be in the least able to fill it. The little boy who seemed to be the same age as one of the girls, her twin perhaps, was crying and wanting mother to get up quickly and make him a pancake.

'Now, my son, I'll make you it quickly,' Frankojannou happened to say.

'We haven't any flour, auntie,' said the elder of the two girls.

'All right. When your father comes and brings the flour,' said Frankojannou to the child, 'I'll make you it quickly. Hush now.'

But the boy would not listen to that.

'I want it quickly and well done and with treacle in.'

'Where shall we get treacle, my son?' said Frankojannou.

'Next week the grapes will get ripe on the vine, and we'll pick them and we'll cut the clusters off the branches, and make lots and lots of treacle for this good little boy to eat. What's your name?'

'He's called Giorgi, auntie,' said the elder of the little girls.

'Yours?'

'Daphno.'

'And yours?' Frankojannou asked the younger girl.

'Anthi.'

'Life to you!'

'And when are we going to cut the grapes, Auntie?' shouted the boy. 'Shall we go to the vines and cut them now?'

'Not now, my son, soon.'

'Soon-soon?' said Giorgi.

'Yes, my little one. Tonight the grapes will swell up and sweeten and darken and soon-soon we'll take the vintagers, and we'll run to the vines, and pick them, and make them mush-mush, the grapes off the clusters, and we'll tread them and mash them and make grape pies and treacle and thousands of nice things, and then I shall make you pancake quickly and well done, maybe in the big pan!'

'I want it very, very big!' said the little boy.

'Quick and big like me,' said Frankojannou.

In the meanwhile Daphno, the smaller of the two girls, was gazing in wonder at the lamp and at Fankojannou, so that she was hypnotized by the old woman's eye and became drowsy. She leant her little head towards the hearth and fell asleep. Frankojannou fondled her persistently under the chin, and sometimes her hand would slip to her throat, and grasp the girl's neck perhaps a little too powerfully. But at that very moment running footsteps were heard from outside, the door opened and in came Kambanachmakis.

'You're here, Mrs Jannou,' he said in great distress. 'Get up! Run away! Hide!'

'What's up?' asked the old woman, trying to appear undisturbed.

'The regulars are after you. Christian woman, what wickedness have you done? The regulars are running along looking for you. Get up, run. Hide somewhere, do. I'm sorry, poor woman. What crime did you do?'

'Me? A lot of them. But I don't know why the regulars are looking for me, like you say.'

'Run. They're coming this way now. I don't know how they a-saw you. However it is, they're close! Listen, in the Black Cave, in the Bad Valley, at the Bird's Spring, if they get anear you there they can't take you. From there you can go down to the Old Man, to the Hermitage, and aconfess your crimes, poor woman. Run.'

The unhappy woman ran, but she no longer felt her full strength. The sleeplessness of the past nights, the bad experiences and the emotions had overcome her. The places Kambanachmakis had mentioned were distant, and she could not journey so far in the moonless night.

As she ran, she constantly strained to listen. She was terrified by the illusion that she heard footsteps everywhere, on the path, among the trees, among the bushes. And then she really did hear footsteps, from two hundred paces away on the main road. She hid behind bushes and it appeared to her that it really was the police moving towards Kambanachmakis' cabin, to the place she had just come from. If that was right, her position was safer at present, since she need have no further fear of coming face to face with them that night.

She went on roughly in the direction she had started out from that morning. She got to the little chapel of the Spring of Life, to the Monks' Cemetery, to the Monastery threshing-ground. She passed outside the Stables, opposite the iron-studded door of the Monastery, which was firmly shut. Anyway, women never entered the holy enclosure. She went down to the gardens where she had met the monk that morning, the gardener monk who had told her the bits of verse from the Psalter. She did not quite know, but she vaguely suspected those verses were somehow fitted to her circumstances. And in fact they had left a kind of booming in her ears. 'Who will give me wings as a dove? . . . Behold I have fled far off and made my abode in the wilderness. I have waited upon God, who saves me from all despairs and from every tempest . . . '

And she came up the ridge opposite, beyond the Gardens, above the brook. She heard the sweet, humble and monotonous chime of the small monastic bell. It woke the echoes of the mountain and shook on the soft breeze. It was midnight then, it was the midnight hour, the matins hour. How fortunate those men were who had felt from their first youth, as if by divine inspiration, what it was best to do and what they could do: not bring other unhappy creatures into the world. Everything was secondary to that. Those men had been granted wisdom as an inheritance, without having to darken their minds with the pursuit of truth which is never captured.

She climbed higher up the ridge without any clear idea where she was going. Off the road, a few steps away, she could see a steading, which she recognized as belonging to Iannis Lyringos. The dog sensed her approach and began to bark.

So she had travelled without thinking, close by her lodging of the previous night! Only now did she begin to consider. Until that moment she had followed her instinct. But now her calculation was clear. 'Where else will I be so safe for the time being? The regulars will never believe I came back to the same place where they found me yesterday and chased after me. Iannis asleep in his sheepfold. The mother and the old woman will be in the cabin. Last night I was in such a panic and such a rush I left my basket there. Wouldn't it be best to go and knock on the door, sell them a service again with some doctoring, fetch my basket, and be off at daybreak to hide down in Bad Valley, where Kambanach-makis was saying? . . .'

Of course the old woman, Lyringos' mother-in-law, would have heard something against her from the police or somebody, but what about it?

She wouldn't be so nasty, nor so bold, as to give her away. Anyway, Frankojannou chief excuse for getting in would be to claim her forgotten basket.

She was very cold from the mountain air and she needed to shelter somewhere for a while. She hesitated no longer. Crossing the neck of land that joined the two ridges, on the more southerly of which the sheepfold was situated, and on the northern one Lyringos' house, she reached the cabin.

She knocked on the door. The old woman was asleep, but she was swift to rise and open the door, without questioning this time who it might be. Maybe she was half asleep and acting mechanically as if she were sleepwalking, or else she had the idea it could be no one else except her son-in-law. Frankojannou got quickly inside.

'I forgot my basket, I was in such a rush yesterday,' she said. 'Have you seen it? Is it anywhere? Where did you put it?'

The old countrywoman stood and looked at her. Only now did she seem to wake up completely and to know her.

'How did you get here?' she said.

'Don't ask,' said Frankojannou. 'I was spending the night in another cabin, but I couldn't sleep. As I remembered my basket, I came. How are you? How's the mother?'

'How would she be? The same . . . But tell me,' said the old woman with a certain hesitation, 'why were those regulars after you?'

'Envy and malice,' Frankojannou replied readily. 'A little girl was drowned in a well.'

'Eh?'

112

'And I don't know what enemy said I was to blame. But by all that's holy, can you believe it? Was the child incapable of drowning on its own? Did I have to have a hand in it?'

'Dear God,' said the old woman.

Frankojannou installed herself as she had done the previous night, close to the corner of the hearth, where she found the basket. She relit the fire, put water in the saucepan, and set to work on the boiling of herbs, which she drew out of her dress.

The mother was asleep, the little girl's breathing was audible from the vessel being used as a cradle, below the barrelhoop that held up a muslin cloth. From time to time she grizzled.

Ki! Ki! Ki!' said the old grandmother, who had shut one eye, and was still watching Frankojannou with the other, by the feeble light of the votive lamp and the uncertain illumination from the hearth.

In the end, although she seemed resolved not to doze off, the old woman was overcome by the traitor sleep – perhaps just because she was staring too persistently at the suspect visitor. She fell asleep at the third crowing of the cock.

The baby was still grizzling. Its grandmother was no longer awake to pronounce that monotonous 'Ki! Ki! Ki!'

'All little girls, the bad luck!' Iannis Lyringos' complaint echoed in Frankojannou's ears.

The mother had not woken. Old Hadoula moved a little, went on hands and knees, and reached the cradle. She removed the muslin above the crib and stretched out her hand to fondle the little one as it grizzled. With one hand she shut the little mouth, so that it should not shout, and she looked where the mother lay, then at the bedding where the old woman lay curled up.

The child's voice choked. Frankojannou needed to use her hand just once more. With her other hand she squeezed the throat hard . . . Then she collected up the muslin to throw it back into place over the barrelhoop. Her hand touched the

113

wood and made a tiny sound. The old woman, who was not deeply asleep, woke up. She woke terrified with a convulsive movement. She saw Frankojannou withdraw her hand and retreat on hands and knees to her place.

'What are you doing?' she shouted in a panic.

The mother woke with a start and jumped up.

'What is it, mother?'

Frankojannou stood up and took her basket.

'Nothing; I wanted to make her nod off and stop crying,' she answered.

The old grandmother bent towards the cradle.

'I'm going now, it's dawn,' said Frankojannou. 'Give the mother a drink of that medicine I boiled up!'

At once she was gone. She raced off to get away as swiftly as possible. She took the upper road through the forest, so as not to pass by the opposite ridge where the sheepfold was.

It was a sweet May dawn. The blue and rose clarity of heaven shed a golden colouring on plants and bushes. The twitter of nightingales could be heard in the woods, and the innumerable small birds uttered their indescribable concert, passionately, insatiably.

When Frankojannou had got some way, she heard a harsh scream behind her. It was the old grandmother; out of her mind, tearing her hair, she had run out of the cabin and shouted:

'Catch her! . . . Catch her! She's done us a murder!'

Frankojannou ran and ran. Her hope was to be swallowed up as soon as possible in the forest, where even if they chanced to run after her, her footprints would be lost at once.

But contrary to her hopes, she came face to face in a few minutes with Iannis Lyringos, who was going towards his house. He had woken at his usual time and he was walking to the cabin, perhaps in order to call his mother-in-law to help with the work, as he had done the previous morning. When he saw his mother-in-law shouting and waving her arms,

114

though he was so far off he was unable to hear what she was saying, he simply followed the direction of her gestures. He saw Frankojannou running away towards the forest. He ran in the same direction and shouted loudly to Frankojannou:

'What is it? . . . What's up?'

At that, Hadoula stopped and shouted back.

'I'm running away. Going to . . . '

Iannis Lyringos had run on several paces and he was coming closer to Frankojannou. At that she too took two or three firm steps towards him.

Frankojannou called all her cunning to help her. She improvised.

'Iannis, your wife has the pains. She's in a bad way.'

'Has the pains!' he yelled in utter helplessness. 'What are you saying, my dear?'

'She has another child in her belly!' Frankojannou assured him with daring.

'Another child in her belly!'

'Yes, what I'm telling you. Just run to the village and call the midwife! . . . And tell the doctor to come!'

Lyringos stood still. Beyond him on the little plateau in front of his house his mother-in-law was still yelling and screaming; the wind carried her cries far, but he could not hear what she was saying. Frankojannou spoke confidently, and she seemed to know what she was talking about.

'However is that?' shouted Iannis. 'Are you in your right wits, my dear?'

'It does happen,' insisted Frankojannou. 'Twins don't always drop together out of the belly, not every time. One of them, that's the weaker one of the two, can wait for hours and for days before it drops.'

'It's true! I've heard of it,' said Iannis.

'It seems,' continued Frankojannou very seriously, 'that this time one of the babies got stuck behind the other.'

'Ah, is that it?' said Lyringos with an air of misery.

115

'Run as quick as you can! Go and get the doctor! . . .'

'Where are you going?' asked Lyringos.

'I'm going to Haji-Haralambo . . . to call Papa Makarios to come and say a prayer for your wife.'

'All right. Run then.'

And Frankojannou ran.

16

———◆———

Down in Bad Valley, in its lowest depths, close to the Black Cave, the rocks were dancing a devil-dance in the night. They stood up like living things, and hunted after Franko-jannou and stoned her, as if they were sling-shot by invisible, avenging hands.

Three days had gone by since her recent flight from Lyringos' cabin. The guilty woman had hidden here in the hope of escaping the talons of her pursuers for a little while. She had survived on the few rusks that were still left in her basket, on the dandelions and wild fennel and chervil that she gathered, and on the brackish water of Black Cave. The place was practically inviolate. The Bad Valley extended from an untrodden rock in the west to a crag and a slippery scree to the east. Down in the bottom the Deadwater bubbled up. Two caverns with very narrow entrances opened one on each side. That was where she slept at night. In the daytime she climbed down to the Black Cave. There was no track or path for her to follow. She clambered over the scree at the foot of the cliff.

Now the scree was disturbed, it seemed to be angry. The stones that she shifted as she walked were a sort of base and foundation for the whole infinite heap of stones that reached to the edge of the cliff. As the first stones were displaced, other stones moved to take their places, and after them came others again. And then the whole tidal wave of the cliff would come down on her, it fell around her thighs and her legs, against her arms and against her breast. At times certain stones dropped from a height and struck with lively malice at her face. It really did feel as if an invisible hand was aiming a sling-shot at her head.

On the first day, when after so much stoning she finally got to the Black Cave, she sat down and contemplated the sea. The sea-beaten Cave had twin entrances, one from dry land, one from the sea. Towards the sea its mouth was low and narrow, just enough to admit a fisherman's small boat. Out of sight from land, Frankojannou listened to the persistent, speechless splashing of waves in the cave-mouth. The waves rose, leapt up, struck the upper lip of the cave-mouth, fell down and leapt up again, with long growls of madness from the open northerly seas, and sometimes a groan of pain and longing from the sea-swell. Down in the untrodden depth, mystery and darkness danced together.

They said a boat had once floated in here after crayfish and sea-turtles. One of the sailors had flung himself up the terrible heights of the rock to gather samphire, but the boat had grounded on a live seal that lay exactly across the breadth of the cave-mouth. The dark creature was disturbed, it heaved. The little boat shook, it trembled, it could go neither back nor forward. The sailor left in the boat struck out at the seal with an axe, he drew blood from it, and the waves crimsoned a little. The seal was shaken with agony. The young sailor managed to get a noose round its head. He yelled to his friend for help. With this help, and in great danger of the dinghy foundering, he did succeed in pulling out the seal.

Old Hadoula gazed and gazed at the sea. If it would appear now, if a boat would come now! . . . Frankojannou would ask the young fishermen, her own fellow villagers, to take her with them in the boat . . . And where would she go? . . . To the lands beyond, the parts over there, the great mainland . . . And what would she do there? Oh, God had it in his hand, she would begin a new life over there!

118

She stared and stared out to sea, far out, at many sails, white sheets like seagulls' wings. Ketches, yawls, little kaikis, she saw them make sail, working the waves like pairs of oxen. Some sailed on to the north, some made southwards, some set sail for the east or the west, crossing one another's trails, the deep, visible furrows of wake that other ships had left behind them. So many streams criss-crossing the sea, so that the surface seemed embroidered, ornamented. She stared on, until her own eyes were distorting glasses.

Frankojannou took out the old yellow woollen blanket that she kept to wrap up in when she wanted sleep and sleep refused to come. She stood up straight, spread out the woollen sheet, and began to shake it passionately. She was making signals, despairing signals, to the sailors to come and take her away with them. Did the sailors see her signals or not? No ship replied to her longing. Nothing answered her efforts. The white sheets fled away with the wind over the waves, and she was left stuck to the rock of the Black Cave, condemned and abandoned. Tomorrow held no vision of golden sunrise.

Her whitish, yellowish rag fled from her hand. The wind took it and flung it round her head and shoulders.

'This will be my winding-sheet,' whispered Frankojannou with a bitter smile.

In the end, as she sat there under the rock, she did see a boat, a little dinghy, come sailing close along the coast. It had a long mast and two oars that struck the sea lazily. It was sailing in from the east, making for the deserted rocks of her sanctuary. Frankojannou felt a hope leap up in her. She hid behind the crest of the rock, safer here to spy and see if she knew the crew. When the dinghy came close, she saw that one of its complement of three, one who was dragging a line from the stern, wore military uniform. Perhaps it was some visiting veteran who loved fishing and had come out for it with two professional sailors. As soon as Frankojannou saw he was a regular, she hid in her disappointment further behind the rock.

She slept in her hiding-place in the dank and brinish cave that night. Echoes boomed in her ears. The waves foamed under her feet with prolonged roars of rage. Deep in her breast, she heard the weeping of innocent infants. Speechless whistles of the distant wind reached her. The dead chorus of little girls, with their frightful necklace now larger, danced and jumped around her: 'We are your children! – You are our mother! – Kiss us! – Give us mmm! – Give us jewels, pretty jewels! – Cuddle us! – Don't you love us?'

Lyringos' old mother-in-law appeared like a madwoman wringing her hands, threatening and terrible; Lyringos himself with his plaintive reproaches. Down at her feet, in the depth of the Cave, the sea broke in foam . . . It boiled and boiled, and the cavern was transformed into a cistern, and the cistern water bellowed in a human voice – Murderess! – Murderess!

The unhappy woman woke shivering, dripping with salt water and sweat. She resolved now never to sleep again in her life, if sleep meant seeing such dreams. Death would be the best of dreams, so long as it was free of such bad dreams! Who knew! She had scarcely formed the thought before she lost consciousness once again. Now she thought she saw Kambanachmakis, the mountain peasant, before her. He stood there with his shepherd's crook, with his awkward manner and rough looks, and spoke to her in his throaty voice: 'At Bad Valley! At the Path, at Birdspring! At the Old Man's Hermitage!'

That disturbed and frightened her. The absence of one policeman was ground for suspicion. Was some ambush waiting for her on the other side of the cliff, beyond the inhospitable rocks of the broken coastline? Would her harsh pursuers have her shut in between two fires?

But again, a coincidence comforted her and inspired her

with a little hope. If one of the two officers of the law was a fellow-villager, a local man in municipal service, that might mean he had undertaken the pursuit he was charged with as an imposition. Perhaps he might delay the mad dash of his companion, the policeman. It was not improbable the field-guard might feel a secret sympathy for the runaway, unfortunate woman that she was, pursued and scrambling up above him with bloody feet on broken rocks. He might not even be quite certain of her guilt.

After some minutes of pursuit, Frankojannou reached the place that Kambanachmakis had called 'the Path on Klima'. It was a rock curving steeply inwards in the shape of a balance-pan. The abyss of the sea yawned below. Near the top there was a ledge a few inches wide. Three or four steps were needed to cross the ledge. To do so, one had to take hold of the rock above, look towards the sea, and balance on one's heels from right to left across the rock-face. Life hung by a hair.

Frankojannou crossed herself and did not hesitate. There was no other choice, no other refuge, no other way round the rock. She took her basket between her teeth, and with resolute movements got over the fearful crossing safely.

The two men of law arrived panting behind her. The policeman saw the crossing-place and stood still.

'How's your courage?' asked his companion with hidden malice.

'There's no other path?'

'No other.'

'You'll have been across here many times,' said the soldier.

'Not me!' answered the field-guard.

'Weren't you a shepherd?'

'I grazed my sheep in the meadows.'

The policeman still hesitated. 'For a woman to do us down!'

'We weren't in time to see her go across,' said the field-

121

guard with irony. 'If you'd seen her it would have given you courage.'

'Really?'

'You don't know how often it's women who set the example!' said the other. 'In some things they show a lot of courage.'

'I'm going across too,' said the policeman.

'Forward!'

The policeman took off his jacket and handed it to his companion. He made the sign of the Cross.

'If I get over, throw it to me,' he said.

He tried a step on the ledge and took hold of the rock. After one step he retreated.

'I got dizzy,' he said.

Meanwhile Frankojannou had run on and climbed up higher to come out on top of the cliffs. She was worn out, panting and gasping. She went on and then for a fleeting moment she strained her ears to listen. She wanted to know whether her two pursuers had crossed over the ledge. But she heard nothing. She thus reckoned that the two officers had hesitated before coming across the Path.

As he disappeared, he went on still: − 'At the Hermitage! At the Old Man's Hermitage!'

Frankojannou woke in the half-light with some degree of peace. The blue and purple of the mainland opposite mingled with the blue-black of the sea. The breeze, the dewfall, the splashing and the birdsong were a sweet harmony to her senses.

Since yesterday she had thought continually of the Hermitage Kambanachmakis had mentioned three days before. She had heard pious women say much of the virtues of that old man, Father Akakios. He had come to the island not long ago and set up at Ayi Sostis, an old retreat with a deserted chapel on a small, sea-lashed rock that constituted a sea-crag, almost a little island, on the steep northern shore, not far to the west. With every ebb of the tide his little island became a small peninsula. Old Father Akakios was said to be a severe confessor. But he had the rare grace of discernment, something amounting to second sight. Other women had assured her he was a real seer of secrets, and he let you know what was inside you. Often he absolved his penitent of much more than the penitent had wanted to confess.

It would have been a piece of luck for Frankojannou, if she indeed had a sincere resolve to confess, to find a confessor who would relieve her of both her burden and the frightful torture of hesitation; one who could say 'You did so and so!' Enough if he did not despair of her, if he was capable of helping her and saving her. Even in this world, if possible! Was there not a Saint who had hidden his own brother's murderer and saved him, refused to betray him to the authorities? How much the more would Father Akakios save her and hide her, since she had done no harm personally to the reverend hermit! Did ships not go by Ayi Sostis every day, heading for the coast or the open sea, and could she not get away if she wanted?

Hadoula was bored with the monotony of the Black Cave. She had also begun to grow weak on her meagre diet. She decided to take her basket and leave her sanctuary as soon as it was properly light, to make for Ayi Sostis. There she would confess all her troubles. It was time to repent.

They had got there, the police had got there! Whether she had been betrayed or tracked down, they had discovered her . . . They had managed to get down into Bad Valley without worrying about the cliff, and even without the stones of the scree rising up and falling on their heads and pursuing them.

It was just as dawn broke, while Frankojannou was getting ready to make by the quickest route for Ayi Sostis, for the Hermitage. The sun had not risen yet to light up the bald shore of Kouroupi, to send its golden rays into the steep cleft of Stivotos.

Frankojannou saw them, and she trembled. She took her

basket and ran uphill gasping, with her tongue out, up to the untrodden rock, to Klima on the west. She flung away her worn out slippers, kicking them off her feet behind her, and barefoot she scrambled up the cliff. The two officers of the law flung off their shoes in their turn, and ran after her up to the unfrequented rock, to the place of despair she was heading for.

Just for one moment, the miserable woman turned her head back. Now she saw that her pursuers were two, but only one of them wore military uniform. The other wore local dress, with a belt of pistols and bullets round his waist. He looked like one of the field guards.

Finally she reached Birdspring, as Kambanachmakis had called it. It was a spring pouring out of high rocks which formed a slippery little plateau covered with earth, full of mosses and water-plants that seemed to be floating in it. Frankojannou stepped carefully so as not to lose her footing. From that spring only the birds of heaven could drink. Hadoula bent and drank . . .

'Ach! As I drink from your spring little birds, grant me your grace to fly away!' And she laughed to herself, unable to imagine how she had thought up a joke at such a moment. But when the birds saw her, they were frightened and fluttered off in a panic . . .

She sat by the Birdspring, to calm herself and catch her breath. She was nearly sure that the two officers of the law had not succeeded in crossing the Path.

Yet the unhappy woman did not feel safe as she sat there. So she rose after a few minutes and took her basket and ran off downhill. Now she was definitely heading for Ayi Sostis, for the Hermitage. It was high time, if she got away, to confess her crimes to the old ascetic.

She was soon down the cliffs and among the pebbles of the seashore and the sand. Opposite to her lay the sea-beaten rock, and on its summit she could see the ancient chapel of the Holy Saviour. The neck of sand linking the isolated rock to the rest of the island stood just an inch above the seawater. It was nearly high tide. Frankojannou stood and hesitated. 'Won't it be low tide again in a little while?' she said. 'Why should I hurry now and get all wet?'

17

At that very moment she heard a fearful clattering on the cliff. Two men, one military and the other civilian, with two guns on their shoulders, were running down the path. The civilian was not the field-guard she had left behind her with the first policeman, it was someone else, and he wore European dress. So this was the ambush she had rightly suspected, the ambush meant to corner her. And look, they had caught up with her.

Frankojannou ran, made the sign of the cross and stepped onto the sandy strip. The sand was slippery. The sea was coming in, it was swelling. She did not draw back. She had no other hope to cling to. Not even this one, by no means this one.

The waves rose higher and higher. Frankojannou went on. The sand gave way. Her feet slid from under her.

The rock of the Holy Saviour was about twenty-five yards from the shore. The neck of sand, the strip, must have been more than fifty paces long.

The waves were round her knees, then up to her waist. The sand gave way, slid. It became a marsh, a pit. The sea was round her breast.

One of the two pursuers fired a shot to frighten her. Then their shouts could be heard, shouts of triumph and certain victory.

Frankojannou was still some twelve paces from Ayi Sostis.

She had no ground left to walk on; she sank to her knees. Salt and bitter water filled her mouth.

Waves swelled up wildly as if angry. They covered her nostrils and her ears. At that moment Frankojannou's eyes turned to Bostani, the deserted northwest shore, where she had been given a field for a dowry when her parents had married her off and set her up.

'Oh, there's my dowry,' she said.

Those were her last words. Old Hadoula met her death at the passage of the Holy Saviour on the neck of sand that links the Hermitage rock with dry land, half-way across, midway between divine and human justice.